I0582446

no such thing

NISSA HARLOW

NIMBLE HOPE
PUBLISHING

Copyright © 2022 by Nissa Harlow

All rights reserved.

No part of this book may be reproduced in any form or by any electronic or mechanical means, including information storage and retrieval systems, without written permission from the author, except for the use of brief quotations in a book review.

Names, characters, businesses, events, locales, and incidents are either the products of the author's imagination or are used in a fictitious manner.

ISBN: 978-1-7777446-8-7

Published in Canada by Nimble Hope Publishing

Cover and book design by Nissa Harlow

For those who are different.
And for those who love them.

· 1 ·

Nice to Meet You

When people see me, their first instinct is to scream.

At least, this is what Dr. Grant tells me. I'm inclined to believe him. Sometimes, if the light is just right, I catch a glimpse of myself in the chrome of a door handle or the reflection of my blank laptop screen. If I didn't know it was me, I would scream, too.

But I'm getting ahead of myself. I've read enough stories and seen enough movies to know that backstory is important. So here's mine. It starts off as stories often do, with four familiar words . . .

Once upon a time, I was a normal little boy. You wouldn't guess it to look at me now, but I was. I lived with my parents in a two-bedroom apartment where the only pet I was allowed to have was a goldfish who went by the name of Gilt. He swam around in a little bowl on my dresser for three years, up until the day I left for good. Knowing what I know now about goldfish, I suspect that the Gilt I left behind was most likely the third or fourth Gilt. Not that my parents ever let me catch on.

Never mind the fish. The point is that I had a pretty normal childhood for my first seven years. I played. I got dirty. I fibbed. I talked back. I had tantrums. I pushed my parents' boundaries, and they, in turn, let me learn about the world around me. Sometimes I had to learn the hard way. But they were almost always fair, and I loved them for it.

Just after my seventh birthday, an old woman came to stay with us. Mom said she was Dad's great aunt, come all the way from some city back east that I'd never heard of. Looking back, I'm not sure why she came to visit us at all, unless it was simply to find someone to take out a lifetime of frustrations on.

When she appeared at the door in a ragged, blue wool coat, smelling of mothballs and stale fish, I immediately backed away and hid behind my mother's legs. The great aunt took off her coat and draped it over my chair at the kitchen table, as if she'd already been living with us for years.

"You," she said. I couldn't see her very well past Mom's legs, but when Dad gently grabbed me by the arm and pulled me out of my hiding spot, I realized the old woman had been talking to me. She shook her head as she took in my appearance. "Too skinny."

"He's fine," Mom said. "Would you like a cup of tea, Adelijda?"

"Dirty," the old woman went on, as if she hadn't heard Mom at all. I glanced down at my jeans. I'd been to the park earlier, and my knees still bore the telltale grass stains of a fun afternoon. "No respect. You should wear clean clothes for visitors."

"I can get the grass stains out of his clothes," Mom said, sounding slightly offended. "I've done it before."

"No!" the woman barked. "No respect for guests."

I looked up in time to see my parents exchange a glance. Seizing the opportunity, I edged backward.

"You like presents?" the woman asked. I stopped in my tracks. Of course I liked presents. What kid didn't? Glancing up at my parents to gauge their reaction, I nodded slowly. The woman clapped her hands together once and reached for the bag she'd plunked on the floor beside the door. When she unzipped it, it released a waft of musty air that reminded me of the alleyway down the street: the one Mom never wanted to walk down because she said we'd probably catch some horrible disease. I leaned against Mom's hip, watching the old woman. Finally, she straightened back up, a crumpled paper bag in her hand. She held it out toward me. As she extended her arm, I caught a glimpse of a faded tattoo on the inside of her wrist. Distorted by age, it was difficult to make out . . . but it looked sort of like a bat with its wings spread wide.

I took the brown bag. It was so damp that it didn't even crinkle as I pulled open the top. More of that nasty smell wafted toward my nose, overpowering the sickly sweet smell of the unwrapped candies within. Most of them were stuck together, lumped into a ball of sugar and . . . whatever the heck that smell was.

"What do you say?" Mom prompted. I closed the bag and clutched the soggy paper in my fist.

"Thank you," I whispered. I couldn't wait to drop the bag. What I really wanted to do was throw it, but I knew that wouldn't go over very well. So I just held it and hoped I wouldn't be expected to sample what was inside.

The old woman huffed. "No kiss?"

My heart stuttered in terror. The last thing I wanted to do was kiss this smelly old woman, and my parents knew it. I'm pretty sure they wouldn't have wanted to kiss her, either. She took a step toward me, and I shook my head hard, my bangs flopping against my forehead. The woman stopped and turned her steely gaze on Mom.

"Such rudeness. You have not taught your son to be kind."

"Sam, give Aunt Adelijda a kiss and tell her thank you," Dad said. I looked up at him in pleading disbelief. He nodded toward the old woman. "Go on."

"I already said thank you."

"Sam, do as you're told."

I looked up at Mom, as if she could save me. She returned my gaze, and, as I saw her expression soften, I felt a surge of relief.

The old woman waited for a few more moments in silence. And then a loud word, in a language I didn't understand, burst from her lips on a wave of disgust.

"Ungrateful little whelp." She eyed the bag of candy as if she were about to snatch it back. As far as I was concerned, she could have it. My hand shaking, I held it out toward her. But she shook her head, and a malevolent smile creased her crackled face. She stepped forward, muttering under her breath in that unfamiliar language, and bent down toward me. Up close, her eyes were like boiled eggs shot through with tiny red lines that continued down the sides of her bulbous nose. A wart wobbled on the edge of her thin, bluish lips. "Do I scare you, little ingrate?"

The question seemed like a trap. If I lied, I would be called on it. So I told the truth.

"Yes."

Her laugh was short and sharp. "Because I am ugly?"

I nodded, my eyes wide. The old woman's eyes narrowed ever so slightly, and the smirk embedded itself on her lips.

"Sam." Mom's quiet voice drifted down from above. "That's not nice. Please say you're sorry to—"

"The time for apologies is over," the old woman said, still staring at me. "Children need to be taught their lessons. And since you have failed at that task, I will help." She brought a claw-like hand under my chin and squeezed my cheeks hard, forcing me to look into her eyes. "You will know what it's like to be reviled. You will learn how it feels to have people shrink from you in terror. I curse you, Samson Woroniecki, to a fate you cannot fathom, and you will know what it is like to be alone. Unless you find a way to break the curse before midnight at the end of your eighteenth birthday—unless you find someone who can love what you are about to become—you will be alone forever." She brought the index finger of her other hand up to my nose and gave it a gentle tap. A spark shot from her hand into my skin with a snap. I jerked back, and she let go of my face.

"Now, just a minute, Aunt Adelijda," Dad said. He looked nervous, but I knew he was trying not to show it. "You're scaring him, and it's not necessary."

"He's just a little boy," Mom added. "He's still learning. We'll work on manners some more. I promise."

"Too late." The old woman chuckled and gathered up her bag and coat. "Where will I sleep?"

And that was the last thought I gave to her words . . . for a few hours, anyway. I stuffed the disgusting bag of candy behind the dresser and fed Gilt while I was at it. His food flakes smelled almost like what was in that paper bag.

Later that night, when Aunt Adelijda was tucked into my bed, breathing her musty old breath into the room, I crawled out of the sleeping bag, fetched the candy, and tip-toed to the bathroom. I meant to flush the candy down the toilet, but it had fused into a lump. I'd learned the hard way the summer before that large objects wouldn't go down (and I'd stupidly left the evidence—a peach with too much fuzz—in the half-flooded bathroom), so I tried to break the candy apart. But it was like cement. Eventually, I gave up and tucked the candy and the bag behind the toilet before heading back toward my room. My head was itchy, like when I'd gotten the chicken pox, and I rubbed furiously at it with my knuckles. A few strands of hair drifted down, tickling the back of my hand. I paused outside my parents' bedroom door. They were talking, but I couldn't hear every-thing. What I did hear, though, sounded angry.

"What gives her the right?" Mom said. "She comes in here, insults my parenting skills, and then scares the crap out of my kid."

"He should've just done as he was told."

"I wasn't about to make him kiss that . . ." Her description of Aunt Adelijda was swallowed by the door. "If she really wants to talk about shortcomings, how about her own? Her hygiene is questionable, and she really doesn't know how to interact with children."

"It's just for a couple of weeks. Then she'll be gone. Hopefully, this is the last trip she'll make out this way."

"Thank god."

"Marianne, keep your voice down."

"I don't care if she hears me. Stupid old bat should take some of her own advice and learn some respect. Just because Sam's a child doesn't give her the right to treat him the way she did." There was a long silence, and then she asked, "Do you think she has dementia?"

"I don't know." Dad's voice was weary. "Maybe. She's old enough."

"Great. Just what we need. You know, I can't believe you agreed to—"

I didn't hear the rest of her words. My stomach clenched so hard that I felt like I'd been punched in the gut, and I bent double, gasping for air. My ears rang, swallowing up my parents' voices. Just when I thought the wave of pain had passed, I was hit by another, this time in my chest. I let out a squeak and fell forward, collapsing against their closed bedroom door. Footsteps reverberated through the floor, and light suddenly poured into the darkened hallway.

"Sam? Sammy, what's wrong?" Mom's gentle hands tried to lift me, but that only made the pain worse. I let out a strangled scream and arched back, kicking my heels against the floor. I grasped my hair in both hands, desperately seeking something to hold on to. It felt like my body was being ripped apart, torn limb from limb by unseen forces. But my grasp was useless as my hair came from my head in huge handfuls, as if nothing had been holding the strands in place at all. "Oh, baby. What's wrong?"

I arched my back and screamed again, my head banging against the floor. My vision seemed to be growing dimmer as well as sharper. I stared up into Mom's face, gasping. She burst into tears of panic.

"Emmett, what's happening? What's happening to him?" She tried to brush her hand through my hair, and more of it came out. She stared at the falling hair, as if she couldn't believe what she was seeing. My body trembled in agony, halfway between waves of pain. Dad swore.

"My god. Look at his skin." I raised my hands and looked down; slowly, but visibly, from the fingertips up, they were turning black.

"What is it?" Mom asked, her voice shaking. "Is it meningitis?"

"I don't know. I don't know." Dad was crying now, too. He lunged for the phone on the bedside table and dialled. "Sam, did you eat any of that candy?"

I wasn't stupid. I wouldn't have eaten any of that candy if it had been the last food on Earth. But I couldn't seem to get the words out. I couldn't even shake my head. I realized, with horror, that another wave of pain was coming. And when it hit, it crashed over me like dark oblivion.

I couldn't breathe. I clawed at my face, feeling like there must've been something covering my nose. But there wasn't. There couldn't be, because my nose was gone, sunk into my face. I opened my mouth wide to take a gasping breath. A scream erupted from me on the exhale.

"Some of us are trying to sleep."

Dad looked up. Aunt Adelijda stood in the doorway to my room, her grey hair standing from her head like steel wool.

"Sam's ill," Dad choked out. "What did you give him? What was in that candy?"

The old woman stared down at me, and the look of cold satisfaction on her face managed to weasel its way into my tortured mind through the curtain of pain. She shook her head slowly.

"It's not the candy."

"You're not a doctor!" Dad shouted. Then he suddenly, quietly, spoke into the phone.

I covered my face with my blackened hands, as if blocking out the world would also make me invisible. Mom hitched me up in her arms, and I leaned against her, trembling and whimpering.

"Hold on, baby. Hold on. Help's coming. They'll be here soon."

I heard Aunt Adelijda snort. "Such fuss. He's not dying."

"Look at him!" Mom cried.

"I suggest you leave him be. You don't want to be too close to him when—"

"When what? When he dies? I'm not going to leave my baby on the cold floor while . . . You heartless old monster. You cruel—"

My shuddering scream cut her off. Pain exploded from my spine, down my arms and legs, shooting through my fingers and toes. I tightened my grip on my face and was rewarded with more pain as something— or, rather, ten sharp somethings—sliced through my flesh. I pulled my hands away and stared. They no longer looked like my hands. My fingers were longer—too long—and there were too many joints. At some point, my fingernails must've fallen off. Now, a needle-like black claw protruded from the end of each digit.

"Marianne, heed my warning." The old woman crouched down and grabbed me under the arms. She tried to pull me away from Mom, out of the only comfort I knew at that horrifying moment. I lashed out, catching Aunt Adelijda across the cheek. Four straight lines cut through her papery skin. It took a moment before they started bleeding. Mom grabbed at my wrist, yelped as my claws nicked her, and tried again for a better grip.

Aunt Adelijda's gaze was cold. "Stupid boy. Do you realize what you've done?" Using the doorframe for support, she slowly creaked to her feet and wobbled back into my bedroom. "Doomed us. Doomed yourself. Don't say I never warned you."

"Mommy." My breath was laboured, coming in violent pants.

"It's okay, baby. It's okay. You're going to be fine." She looked up at Dad, who was still standing there with the forgotten phone. "Where's the ambulance?"

"They're coming." He kept his gaze trained on Mom, as if he couldn't bear to watch what was happening to me. Mom pulled up the hem of my pyjama top. I looked down at my stomach. The skin was an inky black there, too, like it was covered in a charcoal rind.

"Am I going to die?"

She didn't answer. Instead, she pulled me closer and

rocked me back and forth. I grasped her arm, sinking my claws into her skin (which must have hurt, but she didn't say anything), and looked down at my bare feet. My toes had sprouted claws, too, and as I spread them apart, I noticed the fine black webbing stretching between them.

By the time the ambulance arrived, the transformation was really on a roll, and I must've been looking pretty weird. If the webbed toes, claws, and missing nose had been the extent of the transformation, I might have been okay. I might have been able to adapt. But I had no idea that far worse was yet to come.

At the hospital, they rushed me into an isolated trauma room. The doctors had no idea what they were dealing with. For all they knew, I could've been patient zero for a new pandemic plague. I spent the next hour or so strapped to a bed while doctors and nurses in hazmat suits came and went. They tried to start an IV, but they couldn't find a vein. They tried to get me to swallow pills, but I was so terrified that I couldn't keep anything down. And then . . . then the second wave of the transformation hit.

One small mercy is that nobody thought to film the process. They were probably all too busy developing PTSD. From what I've heard, it was the stuff of nightmares, and nobody knew how to explain what had happened. They might have denied it happened at all . . . except I'm here as living proof that it did.

It started with a tingling in my back. Up and down my spine it went, until I was nearly beside myself from wanting to rub at my own skin. Then there was a series of audible pops as my upper spine collapsed and contorted, curving forward and leaving a jagged row of knobs jutting out of my back. I cried out in terror as my nerves were plucked like guitar strings. I tried to sit up to relieve some of the pressure, but there was a strap across my shoulders that held me down. I begged them to let me go, sobbed that I wanted my parents, screamed in wordless panic. But they all stood at a safe distance, watching with wide eyes from behind the presumed safety of their suits.

Once, when I was four, I jumped off the top of the slide at the park and bruised my tailbone. The pain I'd felt then was magnified a hundred—no, a thousand—times as something burst its way out through my skin and bunched under me. I found out later that it was a tail, and although at one time the thought of growing my own tail might've seemed pretty awesome, at that moment . . . it really wasn't.

Then came a similar sensation in my shoulder blades. I pulled and struggled against the restraints, screaming in agony. The pain went on and on, until at last it stopped. Then, there was just discomfort. It felt like I was lying on a pile of sticks. I guess when you've never had wings before, you don't know what they're supposed to feel like.

I lay there, breathing hard, and finally, after a few minutes of silence, one of the doctors approached.

"Is it over?" someone asked. The doctor bent over me. He had a round face, and even through the mask of his suit, I could see that his blond hair was thinning. His glasses reflected some sort of dark shape back at me before he turned away to speak.

"It looks like it."

"Can I see my mom and dad?"

The doctor turned back to me and patted my arm with his heavy glove. "Not just yet. You're a very ill little boy. We don't want them to catch what you've got, do we?"

I shook my head. The motion shot an arrow of pain through my neck, and I gasped. Like tiny fireworks in my mouth, the nerves in my teeth sprang to life. Hot pain flowed into my jaw. I opened my mouth to scream again, and the cry was met by an audible gasp from the watching medical staff. A few of them turned away. I could feel my lips pulling back in an uncontrollable snarl, and then they just weren't there anymore. The bones in my jaw ached, as if someone were stretching them out, pulling them like taffy. I opened my mouth wide, trying to assuage the awful ache. The doctor who had been standing beside me backed away a few paces.

"I want my mom!" But my words sounded nothing like I'd intended. My teeth felt too large, and they clicked like beetles as I clamped them together. "Please. Please." I couldn't make the "p" sound anymore. They didn't understand. How could I make them understand? I moaned and wailed, hoping that seeing my distress would make someone take pity on me and fetch my parents.

It wasn't until hours later that I realized I could no longer cry. My blackened cheeks stayed dry, all through that long first night. They stayed dry even when my father came to visit me the next morning and I pleaded in unintelligible words for him to take me home. He couldn't even look at me, and, after less than a minute, he was gone. My eyes stayed dry even after the round-faced doctor, who told me his name was Dr. Grant, gently informed me that my mother had died. My eyes, black as a lake on a moonless night, have stayed dry ever since.

So. Now you know what I was, and what I am, and how I came to be here at the hospital. I'm sort of a permanent patient, though I'm more of a medical curiosity than someone who needs to be cured.

Although . . . I'm not sure I can be cured.

I'm not sure I care anymore, either way.

• 2 •

They All Scare Easily

I squat on the stool, curling my toes over the edge of the seat. On the desk in front of me, the white rat runs back and forth in its cage, its panic obvious. It knows what's coming.

Lunch has been the same thing for almost eleven years. After Dr. Grant realized that soggy toast and overcooked chicken breast weren't providing me with any nourishment—even when he could get me to eat them—he tried something else, procuring a meal from one of the research labs. It took a bit of coaxing, and though I was sure I would throw up in disgust, I didn't. In fact, the sensation of the warm, wriggling animal's blood spilling into my mouth at the first bite from my razor-sharp teeth was almost enjoyable. Even at the age of seven, I knew I'd crossed a point of no return.

The soft chime and click of the door make me look up. I turn slightly, and the tips of my wings brush against the legs of the stool. The new orderly doesn't look at me as she hurries in, a stack of fresh bedding in her arms, but she knows I'm here. I've never seen her before, but her lack of reaction makes it clear that Dr. Grant has warned her about me, probably shown her some photos and video. He promised to do just that six years ago, after one of the new staffers ended up in the psychiatric wing, wailing about the apocalypse. As far as I know, she's still there.

Ignoring my still-terrified lunch, I edge clockwise on the stool so I can watch the woman. Her purposeful avoidance of my gaze would almost be amusing . . . if it didn't remind me of the fact that I haven't had an intelligent conversation with anyone in almost four days. The online argument about the plausibility of supernatural transformation I got myself into yesterday doesn't really count.

The woman remakes the bed in record time and bunches the dirty sheets (which aren't really that dirty, considering I can't sweat) to her chest. She hurries to the door, still not brave enough to cast a glance in my direction. I cough a little, as if to clear my throat.

"Thank you," I say.

She freezes, her hand pausing halfway to the door handle. Then, slowly, her head turns toward me. Her eyes widen as she sees me crouching there, but I can tell she's trying really hard not to have the sort of reaction that would be . . . well, rude. I cock my head to the side and wiggle my wings against my shoulders, playing it up.

"Would you like to stay for lunch?" As I gesture toward the scurrying rat, a small sob of terror escapes the woman, and she grabs at the door handle, jiggling it desperately.

Someone opens the door from the other side, and she escapes into the hallway. Just before the door closes behind her, I hear her burst into tears.

Crap. I'm going to hear about this later.

As it turns out, "later" is less than ten minutes away. Dr. Grant walks in just as I'm finishing my meal, gulping down the rat's head (I always eat the best part last) with a wheeze that makes the man shudder.

"Tasty?" he asks.

"I've had better."

He sighs. "Sam, what did you do to that poor woman?"

I widen my eyes and try to look innocent, even though I know that expression will have no such effect. "Other than extend a lunch invitation?"

"Don't do that." He smooths his thin blond hair over the top of his shiny pate and shakes his head. "Don't interact. It's hard enough finding willing staff, and I don't like having so many people know about you. It's—"

"—not safe."

"Exactly."

I hop off the stool and stretch up to my full height, which isn't that tall, really. My eyes come up to the level of Dr. Grant's chin. I'd probably be taller if my upper spine weren't all humped and knobbly, but . . . you know. It is what it is. I reach for the gloves on the table, but then think better of it. My hands are still covered in the rat's blood, invisible though it is against my blackened skin. With as much dignity as I can muster, I pull a disinfecting wipe from the canister on the desk and wipe the smears from my fingers.

Dr. Grant leans against the side of the newly made bed,

not quite sitting. He pushes his glasses up his nose and folds his arms across his chest. "You asked to see me?"

I pull on the gloves. They're really quite something, hand sewn from black leather and custom fit to my unusual fingers. Each fingertip is lined with metal and padded with foam, providing the perfect nest for each of my deadly claws. I've had a number of pairs over the years, from a smallish pair for my seven-year-old hands, to the pair I wear now, which must make the glove-maker wonder what his client looks like. I doubt Dr. Grant has given him *that* information, though.

"I'm almost eighteen," I say.

"Yes, Sam. I'm aware of that."

I glance at the desk, where my laptop sits open behind the empty rat cage. "I've been reading about emancipation—"

"Sorry, Sam. You've been reading about what?"

I clench my fists in frustration. I've been repeating myself for years. Losing my lips during the transformation meant losing a number of sounds as well. The word I just spoke sounds more like "enansikation"; I'm not surprised Dr. Grant can't understand me sometimes, but this is one of those times—one of those important times—when I wish he could.

"Emancipation," I say again, hoping the emphasis and the general shape of the word will clue him in. His gaze darkens slightly, and I know he's understood.

"Sam, we've discussed this."

"I'm not a child anymore."

"Where do you think you're going to go? You saw how Trish reacted just now. And I've been showing her photographs and video of you for days, just so what happened today wouldn't happen."

"I can't help it if she scares easily."

"No. I'm sure your behaviour had nothing to do with it." He takes his glasses off, rubs his eyes wearily, and then places them back on his face, settling the nose pads into the reddish divots they've worn into his skin. Glasses sort of fascinate me now. It's not like I need them—actually, according to Dr. Grant, I have better-than-average vision—but I guess I'm just intrigued by something I could never wear myself. It would be kind of hard to wear glasses without a nose or ears to keep them in place.

I reach for the laptop and tap the trackpad to wake it up. "Can I just show you—"

"Sam, I know where this is going. And I'm sorry. I really am. But you can't go out there. It would be dangerous for you. You've watched plenty of movies, read lots of books. What happens when scientists find something they don't understand?"

I keep my gaze on the laptop screen. The government website stares back at me in black and white.

"Sam?"

"They experiment."

"That's right. Do you realize how lucky you are to have ended up where you did? You're still in one piece after eleven years."

"No thanks to you," I mutter.

"What was that?"

I turn to him at last and fold my arms across my chest, mirroring his posture. "So you cut off my wings for fun?"

"No, Sam. I was trying to help you. The amputations of your wings and tail were . . . We thought they would help. We just wanted you to be a normal little boy again."

I let out a huff of air that whistles through my nostril slits. Normal. I've long since given up on normal.

"We didn't know they'd grow back," Dr. Grant says, shaking his head as he remembers. "None of us had ever seen anything like it. Your capacity for healing is . . . unprecedented."

"*I* am unprecedented."

Dr. Grant actually smiles a little. "You are."

"I could hide," I say. "You could take me to one of the parks up north. It's remote. Nobody would see me. And, even if they did, I'd be written off like Bigfoot."

"Sam, Bigfoot isn't real. You are."

I'm tempted to slam the laptop shut. My wings tremble with pent-up anger. "You don't get a say! I'm almost an adult, and—"

"And you're under my care. You're not well."

"I'm not ill."

"Sam, we don't know *what* you are. I want to help you, but I need to know more about you to do that. And I can't learn anything if you go running off to play at being some crypto-zoological phenomenon in the woods."

This is not going well at all. I click my teeth and take a step toward Dr. Grant. "I am not your prisoner!"

"Of course not. But you are my patient. And that means I have a responsibility to protect you. Even if that means protecting you from your own poor choices."

I can't take his smug calmness anymore. I throw my wings wide, letting them tremble with the fury I can feel coursing through me. A growl burbles from my throat, and I open my jaws, giving him an excellent view of my teeth. For good measure, I lick one of my fangs with the tip of my tongue. All Dr. Grant does is raise an eyebrow. I storm toward him and let loose a shriek. It doesn't sound like it should be coming from human vocal cords. The DNA test Dr. Grant ran on me a few years ago says I'm one hundred percent human . . . but anyone who hears the inhuman sound I just made would probably beg to differ.

"Feel better?" Dr. Grant asks. He drops his arms and straightens up, ignoring me as I stand less than a foot away, breathing heavily. He strides to the door and taps on the solid surface to alert the guard on the other side.

"But . . . you can't do this! You can't keep me here. Please. All I want is to go outside. Just once. That can be my birthday present." I look around the room in desperation, seeking some excuse, some way to keep him talking. "What about the curse?"

"Sam." When Dr. Grant turns back to me, the expression on his face is one of derision. He sighs impatiently. "We may not know what caused these changes in you, but I can say with absolute certainty that it was not a curse."

My wings droop as the fight leaves me. I fold them carefully against my back and look down at the floor.

"I know you want it to be something so simple," Dr. Grant says, his voice more gentle now, "because then it would have a simple solution." He taps on the door again, a little more forcefully this time, and it swings open. For a brief moment, I wonder how hard it would be to push past him and make a run for it. Then I remember what happened the last time I dared to try. So I stay put, my feet rooted to the floor, as he walks out. "There's no such thing as curses, Sam." The door closes with a click of finality that punctuates his words.

I stand there for a few minutes, anger roiling in my guts. Or maybe it's the rat that I seem to be having trouble digesting. Finally, I slink over to the bed and lower myself onto it, careful not to sit on the ends of my wings. I curl up on my side and catch a glimpse of my face in the dark screen of my laptop, which has already gone back to sleep.

Dr. Grant is wrong. A curse wouldn't make any of this simple. If anything, it makes it harder. I click my teeth together, watching the grotesque reflection. My eyes glitter darkly, barely visible against my charred-looking face.

There's all sorts of weird stuff on the internet. People have seen strange creatures—or, at least, they claim to have. Mythologies are filled with beings like me. Monsters. Demons. Abominations. They're always viewed the same way: with fear, with loathing, with horror. Nobody ever sees them as anything positive. Nobody ever befriends a monster. Nobody ever falls in love with a demon.

I wish this wasn't a curse. Then maybe Dr. Grant could find a cure. But I know what happened. I remember. I may not have kept much from my old life, but I do have my memories.

No, the fact that this is a curse does not make it simple. All it does is doom me to this existence . . . forever.

And I'll be damned if I'm going to spend that eternity here.

• 3 •

A Pretty Mediocre Jailbreak

I spend the next few hours trying to think up a plan for my escape.

First, I consider disguising myself. But my wings are too difficult to hide, pants tend not to accommodate my tail, and besides . . . asking for clothes after more than a decade of going without would be sure to arouse suspicions. Years of being poked, prodded, and ogled have stripped me of any sort of modesty. If I suddenly ask for a hoodie and jeans, Dr. Grant will know something is up.

Maybe he already knows.

Then, I think that maybe I can overpower the guard outside my door and make my escape. But there are a few problems with that. First, I have no idea where I am in the hospital. My windowless room could be on an upper floor . . . or it could be in the basement. I'll have no idea which way to run, even if I do get past the guard.

Which brings me to the second problem.

Years ago, when Dr. Grant tried to cut off my wings and tail, he quickly discovered that human anaesthesia has no effect on me. The only way they could sedate me enough to even get me to the operating room was to inject me with veterinary tranquilizers. I've been told they're the kind used on large animals like horses. From the way they made me feel, I suspect they're also effective on big game.

Anyway, I found out the hard way that the guard is equipped with a small tranquilizer gun when I made my first—and only—escape attempt a couple of years ago. I made it halfway down the hallway before the stinging dart caught me in the back. By the time I made it to the elevator at the end of the hall, I was on my hands and knees. When I woke up, hours later, I felt like I'd been hit by an elephant, squashed flat under one of its massive feet.

So. That plan is out.

There are a number of vents in my room, and I'm sure they all lead to somewhere, but I have no idea if it's somewhere helpful, or if I'll just topple into a furnace or get chopped up by a fan or get wedged in so tightly I'll end up starving to death. I'd like to see the maintenance staff try to explain finding a demon in the hospital's ductwork.

I crouch in the darkness and curl my toes into the bedsheets. My wings are spread slightly, hanging off the edges of the narrow bed. The rectangle of light in the door is dim, but I know the guard is still there. Someone's always there, though I've never been entirely sure whether that presence is to keep me in or to keep unauthorized others away.

I close my eyes, blocking out the light. I tend to think

better in the dark. Maybe I would have, anyway, even if I hadn't undergone this transformation . . . but I do wonder sometimes if my attraction to darkness and shadows is hardwired into me now. Especially since my brain seems to work better in the absence of any visual stimuli.

My arms are curled around my knees, and, as I rest my jaw against them, I feel the cool edges of my exposed teeth against my skin. I'm careful, wary of the razor-sharp edges that can still surprise me with an injury if I'm not vigilant.

That's when it comes to me.

Do I have the guts to go through with it? I don't know. But it would get me out of this room. I do know that. And once I'm out . . . well, there's no way to predict what will happen, and I'll have to play it by ear. But it's a start. A horrible, gruesome start—I shudder at the thought of what I'm about to do—but it's the only idea I've had that has a chance at succeeding.

I open my eyes and let go of my knees. My heart is pounding. Maybe this isn't such a great idea. But I'm desperate. What other choice do I have? If Dr. Grant has his way, I'll be here until the day I die . . . whenever that might be. I take a deep breath and pull the glove from my right hand. My fingers tremble as I bring them toward my mouth. My jaws open. I slide the unnatural tips of my fingers in between the unnatural teeth. I close my eyes, take another breath.

But I can't do it. My hand falls into my lap as I let out a guttural grunt of disgust. Great. My one idea, and I can't bring myself to go through with it. I pull the glove back on and sit there, letting my pulse calm to its normal rhythm.

It might not have been enough, anyway. Biting off my fingertips would've made me bleed, but perhaps not enough to get me into an operating room. Especially if someone called Dr. Grant. He'd tell them that small wounds like that wouldn't warrant surgery. Not for me. Not when they would heal themselves in a few hours.

As I adjust on the bed, trying to move my tail into a more comfortable position under my body, my wings brush against the sheets. The sound sparks a new idea in my mind. Well, not quite a *new* idea so much as a variation on the previous one.

Even though my wings are just as black as the rest of my skin, in the light, they're kind of translucent. Dark veins and arteries trace maps under the thin membranes of skin. When I was nine, I tried to fly by jumping off the bed. All I ended up doing was breaking my right wing. The bones snapped, puncturing the membrane and tearing through what must've been a major artery, judging by how much blood squirted out onto the wall. Dr. Grant nearly had a heart attack, and he spent the next two hours alternately scolding me and the poor, shell-shocked surgeon who had to patch me up. No doubt the wound would've stopped bleeding on its own, but maybe not soon enough.

I grab my right wing in both hands and pull it forward. My shoulder protests as the muscles and tendons fight back, but if I'm going to be able to reach the blood-rich areas, it's going to be uncomfortable. I turn my head, working the kinks out of my neck, and click my teeth together a few times. For some reason, that movement reminds me of the chef who was sharpening his knife just that afternoon on a TV cooking show. He'd made rabbit stew, cutting up the meat and seasoning it with dill.

What a way to ruin a perfectly good bunny.

"Okay," I whisper into the darkened room, as if the sound of my own voice can impart some courage I'm not really feeling. I pull the wing closer to my mouth. Open my jaws. Take a deep breath. Tell myself to be quick.

The savageness of my own teeth startles me and I drop the wing, the bones of which I've somehow managed to sever. Pain screams in my shoulder as the remains of the wing dangle from the still-intact skin, but I can tell the wing's already healing itself. The flesh tightens and pulls. The cut is too clean. I swear and leap out of the bed, tearing frantically at the other wing with my hands. This time, I don't worry about being quick. I tear into the skin in a frenzy, slicing at it until I can feel slick ribbons of flesh against my tongue. The scent of blood is sharp and heady. I wrench hard, pulling for all I'm worth, and let loose a strangled scream to distract myself from the pain. One quick yank, and the last connection tears apart. The wing drops to the floor with a wet thud. I reach for the other one, which hangs from nothing but a band of skin, its weight tugging against my shoulder. I pull hard, and hear the sick sound of my own flesh tearing. I cast the wing onto the ground, panting in agony.

As I collapse onto the bed, able for the first time in over a decade to lie on my back without being encumbered by those stupid, useless wings, I realize that maybe this isn't so much about escaping the hospital as it is about escaping my life. And, for the briefest of moments, I consider staying quiet. There's a chance I might bleed to death. Then I'd be free.

But I won't have lived. I know what's out there, and I want to experience it for myself. It doesn't seem fair that I should be born, live a mere seven years as a normal boy, be cursed for almost eleven more in the body of a monster, and then die before I have a chance to actually *live*.

And so I scream. I let the sound carry itself out of me, alerting the guard (and probably everyone in close proximity) to the dying monster in the windowless room. I scream again and again, in pain, in fear, in grief. I don't stop when the door opens and the lights come on. I don't stop when I see the blood soaking the sheets and glistening on my gloves. I don't stop when someone calls Dr. Grant, telling him he needs to come right away because Sam is bleeding.

Who is Sam? I have no idea. But I know it's not me. I'm just a monster . . . and I'm dying, whether I want to or not.

· 4 ·

Sorry About the Trauma

A jolt of motion tugs me into consciousness. I open my eyes, but all I can see is blue. There's something covering my face, sucking against my nostrils, making it difficult to breathe. I try to raise my arms to push whatever it is away, but a stab of pain shoots into my back through each shoulder, forcing me to go limp. In a rush, the memory comes back, and my brain slowly makes sense of what's going on.

The scent of blood is trapped under the sheet with me, but it's not as strong as it was before. With my luck, I will have stopped bleeding by the time they get me wherever it is I'm going. I'm on a gurney—I can tell that much by the smooth, rolling motion under me—but I have no idea of the destination. The morgue? Surely they don't think I'm dead. Can't they see me breathing? No, more likely, they just don't want to freak out the whole hospital as we make an unscheduled, unsedated trip to the operating room.

How considerate.

I know I don't have much time. Once we stop and someone takes a good look at my back, they'll realize my wounds are healing fast. I'll be hustled back to my little lair where I can live out my days away from the sensitive souls who can't bear to look at my grotesqueness. Bracing my elbows against the thin padding of the gurney, I press my palms down, ready to spring. My gloves are still on my hands. I guess nobody wanted to chance getting too close to my claws, even if I was unconscious. Probably a wise move.

I'm just about to throw off the sheet when the gurney bumps over some ridges in the floor. I freeze, waiting. A few moments later, I feel the gurney rise against my back.

Great. An elevator.

I have no idea about the layout of the hospital, even though I've lived here most of my life. Like I said, I don't know if my room is in the basement or on one of the upper floors . . . although, if we're going up, that makes the basement more probable. Really, if you think about it, where else would you keep a monster if you had one? Certainly not in the penthouse. If hospitals even have penthouses . . .

I'm starting to wonder if someone gave me a tranquilizer. Maybe I just lost too much blood. Everything feels kind of fuzzy and unreal, like the time I went on a carousel with an undiagnosed ear infection. I kept listing to the right when I tried to walk, and Mom finally had to take me to the doctor. It feels sort of like that now . . . except I didn't even get the enjoyment of the ride.

Finally, the floor stops moving and I'm wheeled out. Even

through the sheet, I can sense the difference in the air. There's a slight hint of something that seeps through the fabric, sharp and clean. It's a smell I recognize from my past, even if the memory is hazy and drugged. I'd know the operating floor anywhere. I also know that, once I'm in that room, they're going to strap me down (for my own safety, as Dr. Grant has told me on more than one occasion), and then I won't get another chance. I suck in a breath through my nostrils, which pulls the sheet against my face.

Now!

I sit up and throw off the sheet in one swift movement. The two nurses pushing the gurney are so stunned that they freeze in place, and I drift a few more feet down the hall, carried by momentum. Someone screams as I tumble off the side of the gurney, landing in a crouch. I look up to see the two nurses backing slowly toward the wall. A burly-looking orderly stands off to my left, his mouth hanging open in shocked horror. Behind him, two doctors in white coats are matching statues. One of them drops the chart in her hands, and it clatters to the floor, overly loud in the suddenly silent hallway.

They didn't send the guard with the nurses. I feel the skin around my mouth pull tighter in what—for me—passes for a smile. Dr. Grant is going to be kicking himself tomorrow. And I wouldn't be surprised if a few people will be out of a job. But that's not my concern. I have other things to worry about at this particular moment.

I rise to my full height, trying to ignore the searing pain in my shoulders. They're healing, but I can feel the scabbing wounds tear back open as I flex my muscles and hunch menacingly toward the orderly. He looks like the one most likely to try to stop me, so I focus my beady black gaze on him and try to put on the best performance of my life. Tilting my head and clicking my teeth, I take another step toward him. He backs up hurriedly, smacking into the two doctors, one of whom is clutching the handset of a phone attached to a nearby nurses' station.

Crap.

I swivel on my heels, turning back to the two nurses who brought me up here. One of them is crying now, her head bowed. The other one can't seem to look away, like a little prey animal trapped in the gaze of the predator who's about to make her his lunch. I have no intention of eating her, but she doesn't know that. One hand makes the sign of the cross, over and over, her fingertips touching forehead, heart, and shoulders. I slide one foot in her direction, and she jumps. Her prayers suddenly become audible.

I look past her to the hallway we just came down. I can see the elevator at the far end, but the doors are closed. There's got to be an emergency staircase nearby.

Looking back at the orderly, who hasn't moved, I let out one of the scariest shrieks I can. If he was getting any ideas about trying to be a hero, they're gone now. I watch as a wet stain darkens the front of his scrubs. Then I turn and make a rush down the hallway.

It's actually pretty easy. Nobody gets in my way. I think a few people actually get concussions from throwing themselves back against the walls so hard; the hollow clunks would make me wince if I weren't so focused on my own desperate need to escape.

I find the stairs to the left of the elevator. My shoulder screams in pain as I push down the handle and throw my body against the door. On the other side, the air is cool and slightly damper than it should be. A giant number four is painted on the wall beside me. Not that that helps much. How many floors does this place have? It's kind of an important question, as I realize I'll have to go up. I can't just go down to the main level and stroll out through the lobby. Too many people have already seen me.

I turn toward the ascending stairs. Despite the pain I'm still in, I manage to take them two at a time. The floors fall away below me, and I keep running. Sixth floor. Seventh floor. Eighth— I come to a crashing halt. No, really. I actually crash into the door on the eighth floor as someone flings it open from the other side and steps into the stairwell. If I had a nose, it would be broken. As it is, I think I might've loosened a few teeth. I throw myself against the door, slamming it closed, and shriek into the face of a very surprised young man in green scrubs. The sound echoes around us, spiralling into the depths of the stairwell. He stumbles back and falls against the stairs, his hands thrown up to protect himself from the creature in front of him.

If I don't make it out of here, if I'm caught and sent back to be Dr. Grant's prisoner, I'm going to be in major trouble.

So. There's only one solution to that: Don't get caught.

I leave the man cowering on the stairs and sprint up two more floors. And then I can't go any farther. The stairs stop. I look at the door beside me, which presumably leads back into the hospital. I look at the door in front of me, which leads . . .

It doesn't matter. The hospital is not an option. I push open the door.

The dark night floods over my body, the air cool and full of sensory input. I let out a gasp and allow the door to fall closed behind me. The surface of the roof is rough under my bare feet. Despite the glow of the lights spaced around the perimeter of the roof, I can see a few stars shining above me.

I fall to my knees, unable to look away, unable to spend the energy to keep myself standing when all I want to do is just stare at the beautiful darkness above me forever. For eleven years, I've had ceilings over my head. Now, the utter endlessness of the sky makes me feel as if I could float away.

And I want to.

I want to so much.

I hunch over and press my hands against the roof. If I had thought this through better, if I hadn't just savaged my own wings, rending them from my body . . . maybe I *could* have floated away. I've never had any success with flying, though. I've never had enough room to practise, even if I hadn't been so busy obeying Dr. Grant's no-flight rule. Maybe my wings don't work. Maybe I'm like a penguin, cursed with useless wings. Maybe they're just for decoration.

The thought makes me want to laugh, but it's a hysterical sort of feeling, and I quash it, worried that if I allow it to emerge, I won't be able to control it. Instead, I get to my feet and walk to the edge.

The outside of the building is clad in brick, which might actually be a good thing. The little joins between the bricks could be just enough to give me hand- and footholds. If not . . . well, I guess I'll find that out when I plummet onto the pavement below.

Carefully, I edge over the side and try to see if I can get a good grip with my toes. I can, but only because they're small and the claws help provide a good grip. But I realize my hands are a different story, especially with the gloves on. I pull myself back up, take off the gloves, and carefully—very carefully—hold them between my teeth. Then I begin my descent.

I'm cloaked in shadows for the first part. Every so often, I look down to try to see how far I have yet to go, but it's hard to tell in the dark. The featureless pavement at the side of the building could be fifty feet away . . . or a hundred. I dig my claws into the bricks, some of which crumble a bit as I put my weight on them. It doesn't give me a lot of confidence in the building's overall integrity.

After a few minutes, I reach the first window. The top edge has a lip, so my toes get to take a bit of a rest for a moment as I balance there to catch my breath. Then, carefully, I swing my body down, letting it dangle over the window. It's dark inside the room, which is a good thing; its occupants are most likely asleep. If not, they're going to get a great view of my naked junk mashed up against the glass. If that happens, I hope they'll write it off as a nightmare.

A few windows—and potential night terrors—later, my arms are trembling violently. As I lower myself from the bottom edge of yet another window to the short expanse of brick below, I hear a shout. I glance up, just as a beam of light sweeps over the edge of the roof, hitting me in the face. I hiss in annoyance and pull myself flat against the side of the building. Why do I bother? They've already seen me. I hear more shouts, and someone yells, "He's on five!"

I glance down at the ground. Five storeys. It's probably a fatal drop. I could keep going, painstakingly making my way down the wall, and have them all waiting for me at the bottom. No. I shake my head, then press my forehead against the bricks. For the second time tonight, I'm going to have to inflict pain on myself. Shouldn't I have some sort of built-in mechanism against that? Maybe it was destroyed when the curse hit.

I take a deep breath, count to three, and let go of the wall.

• 5 •

Maybe I'm Some Sort
of Salamander

The ground rushes up to meet me. Though I can sort of see it in the dark, I can't quite judge the distance, and I hit before I'm expecting it. I try to throw myself to the side, to roll, to try to absorb the force of the blow. But I hear something in my left leg snap. Actually, there's more than one snap. I roll onto my back, my breath coming in gasps. Another beam of light shines down from the roof, sweeping over my broken body.

Damn it, no! They're not going to catch me, take me back, throw me in Dr. Grant's prison. I've had enough of that life. I've had more than enough.

Sitting up, I take stock of my leg. It doesn't look too bad. It hurts like hell, but it's not lying at a funny angle, and no bones have poked through the skin. It's definitely broken, but if I can just have some time to heal, it should be fine. Unfortunately, time isn't on my side tonight. Neither is luck, it seems.

I haul myself closer to the wall of the building, growling at the pain as if to warn it off. There, at the base of the bricks, lie my gloves. I don't even remember dropping them. There's a gash through the leather on the back of one, but that's okay; that's not the part that needs to be intact. I pull them on and rest for a moment, my back pressed against the wall.

My shoulders suddenly lurch and hitch, and I clench my jaws together with such force I'm afraid I might break some teeth. No . . . not now. Damn it! Why couldn't they have grown back when I was on top of the roof?

As quickly as I dare, I drag myself along the wall. Around the corner lies a parking lot and a loading bay. Lights are on, but there's not much activity. It is the middle of the night, after all. Most normal people are sleeping, not chasing demons in the dark . . . or *being* demons in the dark, growing back their wings and trying not to scream from the pain of it all.

There's a white truck sitting between two smaller vans; the logo for a food-supply company is plastered across the side. I drag myself toward it, praying that the voices I hear behind me don't see the dark shadow oozing its way across the parking lot. When I reach the truck, I slide underneath, hunkering down in the shadows of the rear wheels. There's not enough room to sit up, so I do the best I can, trying to manoeuvre my broken leg into a relatively straight position so it can heal. Then I lie back and cover my mouth with my hands to block the screams I know are coming.

This will be the fourth time that wings have grown out of my shoulders. The first time was the worst because I was young and scared and I had no idea what was happening to me. The second time wasn't quite as bad. I understood where the pain was coming from, even if I didn't understand why. The third time was a little bit worse because I realized that, no matter how many times Dr. Grant cut them off, they were going to keep growing back. Luckily, Dr. Grant realized the same thing, and that was the last surgical wingectomy I had to endure.

And that brings us to now. I'm not sure how I feel about it this time. Mostly, I just wish the stupid appendages would hurry up and do their thing. I need to be able to get away, and I can't do it while I'm writhing in agony on the ground.

The jolt of pain hits me again, and this time it feels like someone is trying to wrench my shoulders out of their sockets. I arch my back, my head pressing down against the gritty pavement, and try to hold in the screams. The wave passes, only to be replaced by another . . . and another. My body is really going all out this time. Maybe that's what happens when there's not a surgical cut. I throw my arms out to the sides and bash my fists into the ground, over and over again, bruising my wrists to a pulp, but I don't care as long as it distracts me from the pain in my back, the pain I can't control.

I feel something explode from my shoulders, tearing through the tender, wounded fabric of my skin and unfurling on the ground behind me. I can't help it. The scream bursts out of me, more human than I've heard come out of my body in years. It echoes against the undercarriage of the truck, and I feel a burst of panic. I may have just alerted everyone in the whole hospital to my location.

But nobody comes. I let myself go limp, let my arms fall

back against the leathery membranes of the wings spread out under me. Of course. Of course they're back. I can't change what I am.

I let myself doze, trying to stay half alert to the shout I'm sure to hear at any moment. As the hours pass, the pain in my leg abates somewhat. Still, I'm exhausted. At some point, someone opens the back of the truck and moves around inside. I hear footsteps clomping over my head and something being dragged across the truck's floor. I should pull myself farther into the shadows, but I can't quite muster the energy for that. Instead, I stay as still as I can, hoping I blend in with the darkness.

There's a rumble and a thud above me. Legs appear on my left and walk toward the front of the truck. A door slams. I raise my head, my pulse beginning to race. He's not— Damn it, he is. I startle as the truck roars to life.

If it drives out of here, I'll be exposed, and I have no idea if I'll be able to crawl into a new hiding place before being spotted. My options have dwindled to one.

Carefully, I bend my left knee, drawing my leg toward my body. It's still sore, but it seems solid enough. I look above me, into the shadowy undercarriage of the truck, but I can't see much. So I reach out, feeling with gloved hands for something I can grab. The metal vibrates under my hands, and my arms shake. I don't think I'm up for this. I'm tired, my shoulders are aching, and my stomach is growling. My last meal was more than twelve hours ago. I shake my head and tell myself to forget about that for the time being; I can always grab something on the road.

If I can catch it.

Clenching my teeth, I get a good grip and pull myself up toward the underside of the truck. I raise one foot and feel around, and my toes fumble against a thin bar of metal. I have no idea what it is, but it's just the right shape for me to wrap my toes around. The muscles in my back cry out as I reinforce my grip, trying to keep as much of the front of my body in contact with the truck as I can. I tuck my wings in, holding them so tightly against me that my shoulders cramp.

I don't know how long I'll be able to keep this up. And if I *can't* keep it up, if I lose my grip out there on the streets, I'll be roadkill. Very odd roadkill, but still; it's not the outcome I'm after.

The truck jerks, and then we're moving. I close my eyes and concentrate on keeping myself calm, my fingers and toes locked, the muscles in my limbs taut.

We're probably headed to some sort of warehouse, or an industrial area. But I don't plan on going the whole way. The last thing I want to do is get trapped between concrete buildings, out in the open, with no shadows to hide in.

About half an hour into the ride, my wings scrape against the road. I hiss in agitation and renew my efforts to keep them tightly furled against my body. The last thing I want is to have to regrow them for a second time in one night.

Soon, we're joined by more traffic noise, and when I dare to open my eyes and take a glance to one side, I can see that the shadows look more grey than black. The sun is rising, and it appears we're now a part of the morning commute. Too bad this truck driver doesn't realize he's actually carpooling.

Or maybe he isn't. I'm not sure I count as a second human. The truck takes a swooping turn, probably faster than is wise, and eventually slows. Another glance shows me a stand of trees off to my right. It could be a large swath of parkland . . . but it's hard to tell in this light and from my awkward perspective under the truck. My arms are shaking violently, and though I still have a solid grip with my fingers and toes, my board-stiff posture is threatening to sag. As my wings brush the ground again, I know I'll have to end my ride soon.

The truck rumbles to a stop, but the engine continues to grunt above me. On the left, I can see the wheels and low bodies of other cars, and I realize we're merely at a stoplight. I don't know when I'll have another chance. I pry my fingers from their iron grip and let myself fall onto the pavement.

Before I can roll over and shimmy out from under the truck, it coughs and lurches, and then it's moving again. I watch in panicked disbelief as the undercarriage disappears from above me, and I have a crazy urge to reach out and grab at it again, but I'm too late. The sky above is greyish blue, spread thinly with the last stars of morning. I raise my head just as I hear a squeal of rubber behind me.

I roll over onto my front and push myself to my feet. The driver of the little red car stopped in front of me is young, probably only a few years older than I am. His eyes are wide as he stares at the monster who's still standing there, in the middle of the road, like an idiot. With a practised move that I know looks more animal than human, I shake out my wings, letting the membranes tremble in the early morning air. The man stares at me for a few moments more, then turns his gaze to the paper cup in his hand, as if he's wondering if somebody spiked his morning coffee.

A car horn blasts from somewhere beyond the red car, and I startle. With a shriek that's half surprise and half annoyance, I turn away and bound toward the trees. Out of the corner of my eye, I see the guy drop his coffee and lunge desperately for his steering wheel. My push into the trees is punctuated by the sound of squealing tires as he makes his getaway.

Unfortunately, though the trees provide quite a bit of cover, they don't continue very far. Before long, I come to a chain-link fence, beyond which I can see the back of a neatly kept apartment complex. Wedging myself in between two large trees, couching myself in shadow, I try to catch my breath.

Dr. Grant must know I'm gone by now. I'm sure the people who were chasing me have told him everything. There is a small part of me that feels sort of bad for leaving. After all, Dr. Grant is the only person who's really accepted me since I became . . . this. He's the only one who's never screamed. I'm not sure if he's ever been truly afraid of me. He's a man of science, and I think his curiosity usually overrides his fear. Even when I *try* to scare him, he doesn't take the bait.

I wonder what he's doing now. It's not like he can call the police. What would he say? "My ward has run away and I don't know where to find him. What does he look like? Oh, you know. Blackened skin, wings, tail, poison-secreting claws. A face that'll give you nightmares. Typical teenage boy."

Yeah. That's not going to happen.

So I've probably got a little bit of breathing room. As long as I don't get caught by someone else.

I can see rays of sunlight sparkle through the trees off to my right, and the woods grow brighter with each passing minute. I can't stay here; I need to find someplace to hide.

My leg seems to have mostly healed now. Still, I'm careful as I step through the leaves and twigs, if not for my own safety, then to at least try to stay fairly quiet. Through the open windows of the apartments, I can hear the faint sounds of people getting up and starting the day: mothers scolding their kids to eat their breakfast; the sound of a muffled explosion, which is probably from someone's TV; a baby wailing. I'm so focused on the sounds that I almost don't see the cat until I've stepped on it.

I don't know why it didn't run away when it saw me. Most likely, it was too scared. It stands just a few feet away, its ears plastered back against its head, its yellow-green eyes wide. As I drop into a crouch, it hisses.

I let out a soft chirp. Along with the shriek, the growl, the hiss, and the teeth clicking, it's one of the sounds in my monster repertoire. Probably my favourite one. I figured out I could do it back when I was eight and, as kids are wont to do, practised it until those around me couldn't stand it anymore. Dr. Grant once told me that, to his ears, it has almost the same effect as fingernails on a chalkboard. He shuddered in disgust every time I made the sound, until he finally forbade it.

I'm not sure what the chirp sounds like to the cat, but it definitely doesn't like it. Its grey fur stands on end, making it look almost twice its normal size. It takes a halting, bouncy step back.

"I could eat you," I say, leaning forward to maintain eye contact with the animal. It hisses again. As I feint toward it, it lashes out with one paw, batting harmlessly at my glove before darting away into the trees so quickly that I couldn't follow even if I wanted to.

Which I don't. I draw the line at eating pets.

At the back of the apartment complex, looking kind of out of place, is a small area overgrown with weeds that houses a rusty set of swings, a bent slide, and a rotting playhouse. If this is intended for the younger residents of the complex, they've obviously turned up their noses at it. Quite frankly, I don't blame them.

But it looks like just what I need. I wait a little while in the trees, careful to keep out of view of any of the windows, until the sounds of morning chaos die down. Only then do I sneak from the shadows of the woods and head for the little playhouse.

The door is small, stuck shut with rusty hinges and clogged with weeds, but one good yank manages to get it open. I fold myself into the musty little space, trying to wiggle and adjust my wings so it doesn't feel like the bones are bending. I'm not a huge guy, but the last time I could've comfortably fit in here was probably eleven years ago. Before I was gifted my awkward wings.

The small space only serves to amplify the echoing rumble of my stomach as I doze. The sun heats the playhouse, warming the dry and dusty air. I sneeze once, the sound like a whispering squeak through my nostril slits, and I hold my breath, afraid someone might've heard.

Exhaustion is making me a bit loopy, but I can't let

myself relax enough to sleep. I feel trapped, which I decide is preferable to feeling exposed . . . but only slightly. I rest my head against the rough wooden wall, inhaling the unpleasant scent of untreated wood that's gotten wet one too many times. My eyes close. I tell myself I'm just going to rest them for a moment.

When I startle awake, I can't see a thing. I realize I've slept all day. Cocking my head, angling my right earhole toward the door, I listen. I can't hear much, other than the whispers of leaves and the distant sounds of traffic on the road. Carefully, I nudge the playhouse door open. A few exterior lights are on, but most of the apartment windows are dark. I keep my wings curled around my body as I steal into the night, hoping that, if I'm seen, I'll just be mistaken for a stooped man in an overcoat.

I can hope.

• 6 •

Seventeen Shades of Eigengrau

As I skulk through drainage ditches, I curse Dr. Grant for making any of this necessary. Then I curse myself for daring to curse someone else when I know full well what that sort of thing can lead to.

If he had just agreed to let me go, I wouldn't have had to run away. He could've smuggled me out of the hospital, driven me up to some remote location, and released me into the wild like a rehabilitated bear.

Except I'm not rehabilitated. I don't even think I was ever habilitated. I have no idea what I'm doing. I don't know the first thing about hunting; all of my meals for the last decade have come nicely packaged in shiny metal cages. My stomach is definitely letting me know it's not happy, but I don't know what to do about it. So I growl at it to shut up and hope that nobody sees me talking to myself.

As if *that's* the thing to be worried about.

By the time the sun rises again, I've found myself a nice little culvert to crawl into. It runs under the road, and the metal hums with vibrations every time a vehicle passes overhead. I'm up to my belly button (yes, I still have one; it's an outie, in case you were wondering) in slimy water, but the space is barely large enough for me to sit up in, let alone crouch. My wings are bent awkwardly to fit into the space, the bones bowed slightly as they wedge against the sides of the culvert. It's not quite painful, but I suspect I'm going to feel otherwise by the time the day is over.

In the afternoon, after not seeing any living creatures besides a few insects flying amongst the weeds, I venture out. The skin of my legs feels waterlogged, though it doesn't look any different than it usually does. Maybe a little smoother. When I first arrived at the hospital, Dr. Grant fretted about dehydration. The veins in my arms and hands were too difficult to find, so he ended up placing an IV in one of my wing veins for a while, until he could figure out how I was supposed to drink liquids. Despite the fact that my tongue hadn't changed that much (except for lengthening and tapering to a rather sharp point), the loss of my lips made ingesting any water through the mouth a messy and nearly fruitless endeavour. Drinking with a straw was— and still is—impossible. It wasn't until one of the nurses bathed me about a week into my stay that Dr. Grant realized I could be hydrated through my skin. Like a toad, he said. I asked him if that meant I was cursed like the prince in the story, and that if a pretty girl kissed me, I would turn back into a person. He said no, of course not, and told me it just meant I had a very unique physiology.

Actually, not needing to drink is sort of a perk of my condition. Possibly the only one. It is rather convenient, though. Except, of course, when I've been sitting in water for hours and my legs end up feeling like heavy sponges that need to be wrung out.

So I don't go back into the culvert. I lie down beside it, away from the trickle of water, partially hidden by the tall weeds. My wet skin glistens, looking smooth and shiny, and I notice something I haven't before: My skin isn't actually black. It's *almost* black, but in the sunlight, I can clearly see that it's an extremely dark grey. Eigengrau is the word for it, I think. (How do I know that? Let's just say I have an internet connection and way too much time on my hands.) Not that the colour of my skin is really important. Its water-sucking property still marks me as something . . . well, pretty different.

Who am I kidding? Wings, claws, and a tail aren't exactly run-of-the-mill features for a seventeen-year-old human, either.

Over the years—especially as I've gotten older—I've thought about the things that make me different. That inevitably leads to thoughts about the curse. I can't remember exactly how old I was when I realized that Aunt Adelijda's curse had really fucked up my life. Of course, I always knew the basics: She cursed me, I turned into a monster. Yeah. Got it. But when I was old enough to understand the implications . . . well, let's just say there were certain things that I understood I would never have. All the things I'd taken for granted—that I would grow up, date some girls, maybe fall in love and get married—were just too hard to think about once I realized that guys with tails and fangs aren't exactly in high demand. And I'm sure my lifestyle—living in a basement and eating live rats—isn't going to win me any admirers.

See, this is why I don't like thinking about it. So I push the thoughts of unobtainable girls from my mind, lace my fingers together over my stomach, and close my eyes to snooze in the sun, lulled by the buzz of insects and the burr of cars as they whizz past. If anyone happens to glance over the edge of the road and see me, maybe they'll mistake me for a garbage bag that fell from a passing truck.

When the sky begins to darken, I stand and lumber down the side of the road once more. Beyond the scent of exhaust fumes, there's something else, something that's been building for a while now. It's a fresh scent, coaxed out by the sun and the dew. I can smell the woods long before I see them, and this time, I know it's more than just a few trees.

A small side road cuts in front of me, heading into the woods. I clamber up the embankment and onto the pavement. The gritty surface feels harsh under my feet, which are overly soft from years of smooth hospital floors. The traffic has all but died out, and when I look back the way I came, I can only see one car in the distance. Still, it's coming this way, so I hurry down the small road before it can get too close.

The road opens out into a paved clearing, bordered by trees and lit by lights around the perimeter. The parking lot is nearly empty, save for a pickup truck with a park-services logo on the side. On the far side of the expanse is a kiosk, its roof painted green. I hurry toward it, slipping from shadow to shadow, trying to avoid the pooling lights as much as I can.

The kiosk roof is lit on the underside, casting a yellow glow on the faded trail map. From what I can see, the park is criss-crossed by a number of trails, each numbered and colour-coded. The little red arrow that declares I am "HERE" is scratched and faded, barely visible, but still able to show me I'm at the south end of the park. Most of the trails seem to be concentrated around the south end. My gaze drifts up to the northern trails. A light blue line wends its way around the edge of the map, encircling what looks like a broad expanse of . . . well, I'm not sure what it is. But there aren't any trails running through it—at least, not according to the map—so it looks promising. Making a quick mental note of the name of the light blue trail and how to get there from where I'm currently standing, I lope off into the park.

Dad used to take me on nature walks. We'd spend hours walking the trails in parks similar to this one. Sometimes he'd hold my hand, but near the end of our time together, I'd thought myself too old for that and had insisted on walking by myself. I showed him fallen leaves that looked like misshapen faces and slugs that smeared their way across the path, and he pointed out birds as they swooped overhead and made me listen to their various calls. Mom didn't come with us on those days. She said it was our special "guy time." But I always tried to bring something back for her, whether it was a description of a bird Dad had shown me or the funny rhyme we'd made up about the rabbit we'd seen darting into the bushes.

By the time I reach the marker for the light blue trail, I almost can't see the sign. None of the trails are lit, and

I realize that's why nobody else is here. The park's closed, and I'm trespassing. I don't care. Do the rules even apply to me? I probably have more in common with the snake I can hear slithering through the leaves than with the park maintenance staff who are lurking around here somewhere. If the snake doesn't have to leave when the sun goes down, why should I?

The trail curves around in a sweeping loop, just like I remember from the map. So, if I *am* remembering correctly, then the area off to my right is . . .

What is it? I stop and peer into the trees. I can't see anything unless I look up, and even then it's just a faint image, a black web of branches against a navy-blue expanse. Reaching out my hands to feel for obstacles, I step forward. If I move slowly enough, I might manage to make it into the trees without tripping, falling, and impaling myself on a sharp stick.

Though I have a feeling that would be more painful than fatal.

After about half an hour of scrambling over fallen trees, edging past bushes, getting scratched and snagged in the most inconvenient places (I'm beginning to understand the appeal of pants), I hear the faint trickling sound of water. Was there a stream on the map? It was so faded, it was hard to tell. There might have been. Or maybe it wasn't even marked. In any case, there is some sort of running water nearby, and I'm heading straight for it. My legs barely feel dried out from their last soaking, so I stop where I am and drop into a crouch. Something tickles my tail, and I swipe it away with one hand, hoping it's just a cluster of ferns.

I feel very feral crouching here, and a million miles away from the civilization of the hospital and my sterile room. Digging my toes into the loamy forest floor, I take a deep breath in through my nostrils and let the scents that flow into me draw images from my brain. I remember lying on my stomach in the grass, the dampness soaking through the front of my shirt, as I examined a long-legged spider that crawled between the blades. Another memory surfaces, this one of playing with some other little boys at the park. We didn't even know each other's names, but it didn't matter. We used sticks to dig trenches in the sand, which we piled into fortifications and defended with all the enthusiasm of six-year-old warlords. I remember recess at school in grade one, arguing with the other kids about whose turn it was to use the swings with their sun-warmed plastic seats and smooth chains that always left our hands smelling like metal and dirt.

I longed for school in the first few months after the transformation, but of course I wasn't allowed to go. I'd started grade two just a few months earlier, and I really liked my new teacher. I wonder what they told her had happened to me. I wonder what she'd told my classmates.

Dr. Grant took care of my schooling after that. I'd never considered myself a particularly smart kid, but I guess I was, because I blew through the curriculum and graduated from high school at the age of thirteen. I even started taking some college classes remotely, but eventually gave it up when I realized I'd never be able to use them for anything.

When I was a little kid, before any of this happened, I told my parents I wanted to be a doctor. Dad laughed and told me

I'd better win the lottery if I wanted to do that, but Mom just said I could be anything I wanted to be. I guess she didn't know what fate had in store for me.

Somehow, I don't think Dr. Demon would be very popular with his patients.

Dad never had to worry about affording medical school tuition after the transformation. He never had to worry about me at all. Sometimes I wonder how he could just walk away like that, after seven years of being my father. But then I'll remember what I look like . . . and I understand.

I guess there are limits even for a parent's love.

• 7 •

The Good Stuff Is Always Just Out of Reach

By the time I can see my surroundings the next morning, my knees are stiff, and a spider has managed to string its web between the tip of my left wing and a nearby bush. The spider is nowhere to be seen, which might mean it's off hunting . . . or it's somewhere on my body where I can't feel it. I stand up slowly, expecting to hear an audible crack in my knees, but they stay silent.

The whole area is eerily quiet. The woods are not like I remember at all. I should be hearing birds or scurryings in the underbrush. But there's nothing. The air has gone still, and I can't even hear the leaves whisper against each other. The sound of the running water seems to float in the silence, like it doesn't quite belong. When I spread my wings and give them a good shake to stretch them out and dislodge any friendly spiders, the sound of the membranes slapping against the air seems overly loud. I fold them tightly against my back and step forward through the trees.

There's just a little trickle of a creek a few feet away from where I spent the night. The water sparkles over the pebble-lined bed and glistens on the ferns that dip their fronds toward the coolness. I stop and stand there for a moment, breathing deeply. My sense of smell is no better than the average teenager's, so I don't pick out anything like rabbit pheromones or bird sweat. Do birds sweat? I'll have to look that up sometime. Maybe winged things don't sweat; that would partly explain my skin's dryness.

My stomach feels so empty that I'm sure it must be pressing up against my spine, but when I glance down at my belly, it looks like it usually does. It's not the hollowed-out husk it feels like. I've never gone this long without eating before. It's been . . . I don't know how long. I'm hungry, and I can't think very well when I'm hungry. It's been a couple of days since my last rat, anyway.

I crouch by the edge of the stream. Most animals need to drink, right? So something—something I can eat—should come along sooner or later. I just need to be prepared. I slip off my gloves and lay them neatly on a nearby stump, then go still as I wait.

And wait.

And wait.

Until I realize that I may not be able to sense any animals around me, but they're almost certainly sensing me and wisely keeping their distance. I bet I smell like danger. Or hunger. In any case, nothing with any sort of survival instinct is going to come anywhere near me.

I let out an experimental chirp, then startle as it's answered from somewhere high above my head. I look up just in time to see a flash of movement, brown wings darting between the trees and disappearing amongst the leaves. My wings tremble, as if they long to stretch and flap and take me up into the treetops.

Useless instinct. Useless flaps of flesh and bone.

With a growl that's half despair and half pure hunger, I stand up and storm through the creek, splashing icy water nearly to my knees. Gripping the nearest tree trunk with my claws, I shimmy up a few feet. It's easier than I expected, and, with a sudden burst of hope, I think about nests full of eggs or—if I'm lucky—helpless baby birds. But . . . it's October. The babies will all be grown, and any nests I might find up there are likely to be empty. Dejected, I let myself slide back to the ground. Before I turn away, I take an angry swipe at the tree, and my claws leave four parallel gashes through the delicate-looking bark.

I should have thought about all of this before I left the relative comfort of the hospital. But, let's face it: I wasn't really thinking. The thought that I'm an impulsive idiot, just like many human teenagers, might provide a small measure of comfort if I weren't so pissed off at myself.

What did I think would happen? That I would come and live this idyllic life in the woods and magically know how to hunt? I guess I sort of hoped that would be the case, that some sort of natural hunting instinct would kick in and I would be up to my eyeballs in fresh meat. What I didn't count on was not even *seeing* any fresh meat. It's probably some sort of failsafe, a way of forcing me to starve to death, nature's way of correcting the mistake that is me.

I cross back to the stream and crouch down, letting the water run over everything that's dangling into it. My fingers play idly with the smooth pebbles under the surface, flicking them from side to side. I watch the extra-jointed digits curl and move, and am more fascinated by the fact that I have control over them than the fact that they're there in the first place. Dr. Grant was amazed I adapted to my new hands so quickly. I was playing video games within a couple of weeks of the transformation and beating him a few days after that. Mind you, Dr. Grant sucks at every game, so that's not actually saying much.

Maybe I should go back. I know he'd let me return. He didn't want me to go in the first place. I can go back, and he can draw my blood and run his tests; remove my wings again and hope that *this time* it'll take; extract all my horrible teeth and reconstruct my jaw, and try not to show frustration when it turns out that the hours of surgery have all been for nothing. And I will lie there and pretend I don't care about the pain he's putting me through. I will pretend I believe him when he says he's hopeful that *this time* one of the treatments will work.

Screw that. I'm sick of pretending.

None of Dr. Grant's treatments work. None of them will ever work. He thinks I have some sort of disease, something that can be seen if he just runs enough tests and scans me enough times. He'll never see what's really going on, because he doesn't want to see it.

I'm not sure he even can.

I sit down in the creek and stretch my legs out in front of me, spreading my toes and letting the water splash over the webbing. I scoop handfuls of water and wash down my arms, my torso, and the parts of my wings I can reach, ridding them of the grime from my journey that I can't see against the darkness of my skin, but that I know is there nonetheless. I rub my wet hands over my head, feeling the smooth, featureless surface of my scalp, the hairless brow and eyelids, the jawbone that is just a little too long for a human.

I'm not human anymore. That's what Dr. Grant doesn't understand. He wants me to be as I was, but all I can be is what I am. As I feel the contours of my head, I realize this, and I know that, curse or no curse, this is the body I will spend the rest of my life in. Humans can't accept something that looks like this. Like me. I don't belong with them. That was Dr. Grant's aim with all his treatments, I suppose: to make me belong.

But it's futile.

When I'm done with my little bath, I sit there for a few moments longer, until I'm afraid the cold water is going to make my balls shrivel up and fall off. Then I stand, shake the water from my body like an animal, and pick up my gloves before moving farther into the trees.

Smells Like Chicken

I t's pretty here, but I'm so hungry I barely notice. After spending the morning skulking through the bushes and making a couple of hikers think they caught a glimpse of a very ill bear—which, I have to admit, *was* kind of funny— I've gotten a better idea of the layout of my surroundings. Aside from the small creek, there's nothing of note in this portion of park that's encircled by the light blue trail. I'd like to explore the land on the other side of the trail, but I'm afraid to try to cross. Nobody's "bear aware," as the signs on the trail warn, and none of the walkers are making enough noise to warn off the wildlife—which includes me. I've already been spotted once. I don't particularly want to be seen again.

So I hunker down behind a tall tree stump and its still-intact neighbour. Between the two, I have a good view of the trail, but I probably can't be seen. If someone were to look really close, they might see one of my black eyes staring back out at them, but nobody appears to be that observant . . . or that interested. The hikers are all too busy playing with the step-counting gadgets on their wrists, drinking from fancy water bottles, and—for the couples, anyway—holding hands. The sight makes a low growl rumble from somewhere deep within me. I have a sudden urge to tear off those clasping hands and eat them, step-counters and all.

But that would probably just give me indigestion.

Late in the afternoon, I decide to take a chance. My knees are cramped again, and I'm bored out of my mind. If I have to watch one more potential meal prance by in stretchy pants, I think I'm going to scream.

I tell myself to calm down. I don't eat people. Although, if I get any hungrier, who knows what I might do?

The trail is empty as I pull myself from the cover of the forest. Without even waiting to look either way, I dash across and plunge into the trees on the other side. My relief gives me a burst of endorphins that propels me farther into the trees. I run, leaping over logs, scrambling on hands and feet up slopes of pine needles, my wings furled tightly against my back to avoid getting caught on the branches that I have to duck and dodge as I move through the trees. I've lost all sense of direction, so I have no idea what part of the park I'm in now. I certainly don't remember there being this much space on the other side of the light blue trail . . . but, then again, it was a long, curving path, and I'm not sure what part of it I crossed.

Screw the map. Maps are for humans. I don't need to

know where to go, as long as it leads me somewhere that'll satisfy my needs.

The light is fading fast, but, even so, I can see the trees thin out up ahead. I pass the last of them and stagger to a stop at the edge of a field. The land here is fairly flat, though I can see some hills rising in the distance, silhouetted against the orange-and-pink sky. The expanse is broken only by a few stands of trees. There's one to my left, which looks much like the one I just emerged from. Almost directly in front of me lies another. Tucked into the edge are a couple of buildings: a two-storey house and a one-storey building with a flat roof that I can't quite see past all the trees. A barn? My mouth starts to water. I can't help myself. Saliva oozes out from between my teeth and dangles there in a sticky strand. I leave it as I run toward the buildings, and it slaps back against my face.

Closer, I can smell . . . something. It's an animal smell, slightly unpleasant. Like the manure our landlord used to put on the front gardens of the apartment building. Ridiculously, the smell only makes my slavering worse. My body recognizes—long before my conscious mind does—that where there's crap, there's something producing that crap.

The barn—because it *is* a barn—looks pretty rough close up. The grey walls are worn and rough, the wood so old that the colour might be from paint or simply from age; it's hard to tell in the dim light. The nearest window is cracked, held together by a yellowed piece of masking tape. I slink up to it and raise my head, trying to peer inside. It's too dark to see much other than the light coming from the other windows and from around the door on the opposite wall, but there's no light leaking in from above, so the roof is at least in better shape than the walls. I duck back down and creep around the corner. A low fence blocks my way. I step over the chicken wire, lifting my wings so they don't snag, then settling them against my back once more. I hope that the presence of chicken wire is a good sign.

It is. It's a very good sign. I hear them before I see them, or even smell them. The coop is nestled against the front of the barn, near the door. A few of the birds are poking about, oblivious to the hungry beast watching from the shadows. My teeth click together as my jaw spasms in solidarity with my stomach.

And the birds go nuts.

There's a frenzy of flapping and feathers, and I bet you had no idea that chickens could scream, but they can. Or, at least, they come close. I draw back around the side of the barn, my heart pounding, as a light flashes on just outside the back door of the house, and I hear hinges creak.

"Damn birds. Mija, did you close the—" The voice breaks off, and I hear a whispered swear. I'm pretty sure I can't be seen in the shadows, but I flatten myself against the wall of the barn anyway, until my wing bones dig into my ribs.

"Dad?" The young female voice startles me. I desperately want to look—after all, I haven't seen many people my own age in the last decade—but I know that's probably not a good idea. The girl's father whispers something, his voice hushed and reverent . . . and a little bit scared. Crap. Did he see me?

"Dad. Seriously? It's just a shadow. There's no such thing." There's the sound of footsteps, like someone coming down wooden stairs.

"No, mija."

"Do you want them all running away during the night? I haven't closed the coop yet. Just let me—"

"No. I'll do it."

"They're my responsibility, remember?"

"Take the gun, then."

The girl groans, and I imagine her rolling her eyes.

"It might be a bear," the man says. The girl is silent. Finally, I hear the door close and a set of soft footsteps approaching.

I would be lying if I said this doesn't concern me. My head is spinning from hunger, from adrenaline, and the smell of those clucking featherballs is *not* helping. If the girl finds me, what will she do? What will *I* do?

I hear her gentle voice coaxing the birds back where they're supposed to be, soothing the panicked fowl. The chickens are still clucking, but the sound is softer now as they start to settle down. After a few minutes, there's a metallic clunk. It reminds me of the latch on the rat cages that arrived in my room every day at noon. I sit and wait, still pressed against the wall. The shadows are falling quickly now, blanketing the yard in darkness. I didn't hear the girl go back into the house, but I don't hear footsteps or breathing or any other signs of life—other than the soft clucking of the birds as they settle for the night—so I assume she did. Slowly, I lean forward and peer around the corner. The yard is empty.

Sending a silent word of thanks to the girl—wherever she is—for making the job of obtaining dinner easier, I slink toward the coop. The birds sense my presence when

I'm only a few feet away and start panicking again. I pause. This is going to have to be quick. Eyeing the latch, I try to calculate how best to go about it. Maybe I should just rip off the door. But then I might find myself up against a replacement that's much harder to foil. And I *will* be coming back. There've got to be nearly a dozen chickens in there, and I'm not about to walk away from such easy pickings.

I take a deep breath in through my nostrils and try to ignore the burst of alarm the whistle seems to send through the coop. I rush forward, grab the latch, and pull. It's a simple mechanism (thank goodness), and a moment later I've got my hand on the door itself.

"Hey!"

Before I can stop myself, I turn toward the source of the voice. The girl stands in the open doorway to the barn. My wings tremble as a potent mixture of fear and fury courses through me. To come so close to a meal after so many days without so much as a snack, only to be thwarted . . . I can't bear it. My teeth click twice, and I open my mouth wide as I straighten up, unfurling my wings. Quick as a flash, the girl moves, and in the split second it takes for me to realize she's raising a rifle to her shoulder, I simultaneously realize I've made a horrible mistake.

The gun goes off in an explosion of pain and sound, and I fall back against the coop, scaring the chickens beyond all reason and catching my head on a hard corner. My body slumps to the ground, crushing my wings under me, and I'm left staring up at the spangled sky.

· 9 ·

Ow

The girl is an idiot. She has to be. Any sane person would run away after encountering something like me in her backyard. Instead, she's edging toward me, gun at the ready, peering down at the shadow creature on the ground. I push back with my feet, trying to move away from her and sit up at the same time, which doesn't work very well. My left shoulder is bleeding, black chunks of flesh flayed open around the wound. In a daze, I wonder if my body will be able to recover from *that*. I let my head fall back, and it comes to rest on one of my wings, which are bent awkwardly beneath me.

The girl steps closer, and I let out a hiss that makes her pause.

"Omigod," she breathes, in a way I've only ever heard on TV, the words all running together into one. Her gaze sweeps over me, taking in my skin, my teeth, my wings, before settling on the glistening wound. A flash of something passes over her features, and she turns her gaze back to my eyes. I click my teeth and try to raise my head.

"Stay back," I say.

"Omigod." She looks back at the house, and it takes a moment before I realize why. Another figure is hurtling toward us, his dark hair wild in the breeze of his head-long rush. "Dad! He's—"

He doesn't wait for her to finish. He grabs the rifle from her hands, turns, aims, and pulls the trigger. The concussive force of the shot hammers my body into the ground.

This is it. I'm dying.

"Dad, stop!" The girl's tearful voice cuts through the pain. I can't move. My heart is pulsing hard, beating through the fiery agony of where the blast hit me in the chest. I'm not sure if I'm dazed, if I'm in shock, or if something necessary for life has been hit. Maybe I'm already dead. I'm pretty sure I'm not, though. I don't think being dead is supposed to hurt so much.

"Go into the house, mija. Go!"

"Dad, he talked!"

Her father grunts. "A creature like that can't talk."

"Yes, it can. And now you've killed him."

"Better the monster than my chickens."

"*My* chickens," the girl says.

"Doesn't matter. It's dead now." He steps closer and stares down at me. As his gaze sweeps over my jaw, he shudders. Turning, he hands the gun to the girl. "Go into the house. I'll deal with this."

"Dad!" The girl sounds shocked, disgusted. "You have to call someone! You just killed—"

"A monster," he says. "It's a monster, mija. Who should I call? The ambulance?" He shakes his head with another grunt. "No. We deal with this ourselves. We'll burn the body. Send it back to hell where it came from."

Crap.

He snorts and spits onto my prone form. I try not to flinch.

"Dad. Stop it." The girl's face contorts as she starts to cry. The gun hangs from her hands, forgotten. "He was probably just hungry. You didn't need to . . ." She trails off, and the man walks back to her. He puts his arms around her shoulders, pulls her close.

"We do this quick, all right? There's gasoline in the barn, and we can burn it in the fire pit."

Crap. Oh, *crap*.

The girl pulls away and wipes her cheeks with the back of one hand. "I could've sworn he talked."

"If it did, then it really is unnatural. We need to get rid of it before the body attracts more of its kind." He nods at the house as he moves toward the side of the barn. "You don't have to help me. I can do it myself."

The girl nods, watching him go. Then she turns back to me.

My fingers twitch, and I realize I can move again. But I don't. I'm still alive—albeit barely—and she's still holding the gun. The last thing I want to do is startle her into a reflex.

"I'm sorry," she says. She steps close, so close I can feel her shoe against the edge of one of my wings. I turn my eyes to look at her, but she doesn't seem to notice the movement. To my horror, she crouches down and balances the gun across her knees. Her dark braid slips over her shoulder as she leans closer. I can see sadness in her eyes, and regret. Guilt. Why? She was just protecting her chickens. And I *was* about to steal one of them.

As if in slow motion, she reaches one hand toward me. Her skin is smooth and tan, and looks so delicate. Her hand pauses on its way to the wound on my chest, then changes direction, moving higher. I stop breathing. Her finger brushes against my face, just above my teeth, where my upper lip used to be.

"No," I say. "Be careful."

The girl gasps and draws her hand away. She glances over her shoulder, then turns back to me.

"You're alive?"

"Not for long."

"No kidding," she whispers. "You've got to get out of here. Now. Before my dad gets back. You know what he's going to do, right?"

I know. But I'm not sure there's anything I can do to stop it. My muscles are weak and exhausted. Healing is a draining endeavour, and I've had to do it too many times now with no fuel. I let out a whistling breath through my nostrils. The girl darts a glance at the slits, then casts the gun on the ground.

"Come on," she says, reaching for me as if to help me up. I click my teeth at her, and she draws back.

Clenching my jaw, I roll over and push myself up onto my hands and knees. Shadows crowd in at the corners of my vision.

"Hurry! He's coming back."

I hang my head. My wings droop over my body like a limp blanket. Where am I supposed to go? How am I supposed to get there? I'm too weak. Too weak, too tired, too hungry, too injured. I can sense the girl hovering, her unease palpable.

"I'll try to slow him down. Just . . . go. Please." Her footsteps retreat into the night.

I'm so tempted to just lie down and let her father light the match. Could being burned to death be any worse than some of the things I've already gone through?

I'm not ready to find out.

Pushing myself up on unsteady legs, I take a staggering step, then another, nearly sprawling on the ground as I try to step over the low, chicken-wire fencing. I have no idea where I'm going. I just want it to be someplace dark, somewhere I can hide, somewhere I can die in peace, if it comes to that.

By the time I collapse onto my wounds in a pine-scented clearing, I can hear the distant sounds of the girl and her father shouting. I hope she's not in trouble for saving my sorry ass.

I'm hardly worth it.

• 10 •

Not Very Bright

The smell of blood, even though it's my own, makes my stomach clench in agony, adding to the immense amount of pain I'm already in. I can feel the flesh on my shoulder pulling, tightening, as it heals itself. It's too dark to see anything, but I know the wound isn't what it was even just a few minutes ago. The hole in my chest seems to be taking a bit longer, though I don't even want to know what's going on there. The blast obviously missed my heart, but there must've been some damage. I'm afraid to even explore with my fingers to find out how much.

I lie on my right side, wings spread limply on the ground behind me, as I wait for my body to patch itself up. A horrible thought that's been niggling in the corner of my mind finally pushes its way into my consciousness. I growl softly at it, as if that might make it run back and cower in its corner. But it's an insistent little thing, and I don't have the strength to fight it anymore.

Being cursed to live in this body is one thing. But knowing that it might be forever? That's another. I have no idea how long I might live. My growth and development seems to be on par with a normal human being . . . so far. I went through puberty in my early teens, even if all that meant was the deepening of my voice, the growth of the organs between my legs (that I'll never get to use), and a massive growth spurt that Dr. Grant seemed to think I had on purpose, just to spite him; I went through three pairs of gloves in six months alone.

But my body can do something that most human bodies can't: It can heal itself from injuries that should, by all rights, kill it. If that's going on—at a much smaller level— on the inside, if my body is repairing damage before I even know it's there, what does that mean for my aging? What's my lifespan? Will I live to eighty, like my grandfather? Ninety? One hundred?

More?

Forever?

Immortality is one of those things that sounds great until you're actually faced with it. What would it be like to live forever, if you were the only one who could? You'd have to say goodbye to everyone you loved, eventually. You'd go into every relationship knowing it was only temporary. Maybe you'd withdraw from the world just to protect yourself.

Maybe you'd withdraw from the world just to protect everyone else.

I realize I'm breathing hard, my nostrils making quite

the whistling racket. The healing is taking longer than it usually does. I know why, too. My body is spent. It's hungry. It's tired.

So am I.

I curl my legs toward my chest and press the palms of my gloved hands over my eyes. The pain swirls through my wounds, but I try to concentrate on my breathing, willing the air in and out of my lungs, as if it can give me the sustenance I need. Within an hour or two, I feel weaker than ever, but the pain has begun to subside. My hands fall to the ground in front of my face. As the soft ticking sound on the leaves above me heralds the beginning of a gentle rain, I pull my left wing over my body, protecting the still-healing wounds. The darkness cocoons me, and I close my eyes, letting myself drift toward sleep.

I feel damp.

When I open my eyes, the light is dim under the cover of the trees, but I can see my surroundings with perfect clarity. A fine drizzle hangs in the air, more mist than rain. I get up onto my knees, shaking the gathered raindrops from my wings.

The skin on my shoulder and chest is smooth and unmarked, as if nothing happened last night. I can see a thin, dark film smeared across the flesh, the only clue that I didn't imagine the whole thing. I rub at it with my gloved hand, using the dampness of the mist to my benefit. The film thins a bit, but persists. It's going to take more than a quick mist bath to rid my body of the remains of *that* near-death experience.

I look around but can't see anything but trees, bushes, and a white mist that lingers above my head in the treetops. Disoriented, I try to recall which way I was lying, as if that'll help me remember which way I entered the clearing. I shake my head to clear it and am hit with a wave of dizziness. How much blood did I lose? Not enough to kill me, I guess. Still, as I get up on shaking legs, I do wonder if I might've come close.

There's a low rumbling coming from somewhere, and I turn in a slow circle, searching for the source of the sound. When I realize it's me, I let the growl turn into a bark, then a shriek. Enough is enough. I have to eat. Now.

Do I care that it's fully daylight and anyone could see me? Do I care that there's a father and daughter nearby who are both equally adept at using a really big gun? Do I care that this meal I'm determined to eat could be my last?

No. I'm beyond caring. If I wasn't already a beast before, I surely am now, driven nearly mad with the gnawing pain in my belly, the giddy weakness in my limbs. Logical thought has gone out the window, along with any sort of prudence. I crash through the trees, grabbing at trunks and low-hanging branches, tearing at bushes in my wild, animal frustration. Another shriek tears out of my throat as I throw myself forward, desperately searching for something I can sink my teeth into.

Dark shadows press in on my vision, narrowing it to a fine point directly in front of me. I tear past a bush that tries to attack me with rows of sharp little claws of its own, ripping half of it out of the ground as I go. My foot catches. I stumble forward and fall, my wrists jarring as I hit the hard dirt. There's a burst of excited clucking. A feathered wing slaps against my head as a bird hastily retreats from where I lie on the ground. I blink, and the relief of having food so close allows the darkness to retreat a little.

That's when I see her.

She stares. At least she doesn't scream. Why isn't she screaming? She can see everything now. Everything I am. Every horrible inch of me. But she's quiet. Her dark hair is in a messy ponytail today, and she's wearing a pair of rubber boots over her pyjamas, like she threw them on and rushed out here. Which she probably did.

Even though I'm not sure I can, I attempt to stand. When I'm up, I wobble once and throw out my hand for balance, which probably makes me look more pathetic than menacing. I straighten up to my full height, noticing that, even with my hunched back, I'm still slightly taller than her.

The chickens have all retreated to one corner of the fenced yard, like soap bubbles caught in a current. I gaze at them longingly, and my teeth click as I imagine sinking them into the plump, bloody flesh.

"You may be able to talk, but you're obviously not very bright."

I whip my head toward the girl. She startles a little at the sudden movement, but recovers quickly, folding her arms across her chest and raising her chin.

"Bright," I repeat slowly.

"You're lucky my dad had an early shift this morning. If he saw you come back, he'd blow your head off. Do you have a death wish?"

"Yes." I consider her, tilting my head and taking in a long breath. She smells like something familiar, but I can't quite place it.

"'Yes?' You *want* my father to shoot you?"

I shrug my shoulders, which makes my wings rustle. My attention is drawn once more to the mass of feathers and fretting. Talk about shooting fish in a barrel. Or grabbing chickens in a corner, I guess. I take a step toward them, forgetting about the girl until she speaks again.

"Did you come back to get shot or to steal my chickens?"

"Chickens," I reply without taking my gaze from the birds. "But only one of them." There's a brown speckled hen wedged in the corner that looks particularly appetizing. As I step forward and sweep my arm down, ready to grab, the ball of clucking explodes once more. The birds scatter, and I'm left with nothing but a handful of feathers.

"Omigod."

I look back, and when I see the expression on her face, it hits me harder than that first shot she took at me with her gun.

She's not frightened. She's not even angry.

She's *laughing*. At me.

"You're going to have to try harder than that," she says with a giggle. It's such a beautiful sound, so unfamiliar and special, a sound I haven't heard in my vicinity in almost eleven years, that all I can do is stand there and gape. My mouth is hanging open, and what for any other teenage boy would look like a dumbfounded expression is probably pretty menacing on me, what with all the teeth. But she doesn't seem to notice. She looks at the chickens running crazily around my feet, then at the handful of brown feathers still clutched in my gloved hand, and shakes her head with another laugh. This time, my body responds of its own accord. I let the feathers fall from my hand as I stand there on full display, hot shame creeping into every corner of my dark little heart. Despite the fact that I find them extremely uncomfortable, at this moment I'm desperately wishing for a pair of pants. Although, I suspect that even a pair of baggy cargo pants wouldn't be able to disguise what's going on between my legs.

The girl's laughter dies as her gaze drifts down. She takes a step back, for the first time, it seems, afraid.

"I'm sorry." My feet walk me backward, away from the chickens, back toward the gap in the fence I created when I crashed through. My stomach is wailing in agony, but my mortification is strong enough to override everything. I stumble back over the bent wire, turning my out-of-control body away from her before plunging into the trees.

• 11 •

Sorry, Linda

When I'm far enough away and my stupid body has stopped trying to kill me with embarrassment, I tear off my gloves and attack the nearest tree. Shrieking with rage and frustration, I throw my hands at it, try to tear the bark off with my claws, attempt to push it over. When that proves to be less than satisfying, I turn my attention to the bushes instead. The roots come up from the ground with a rewarding series of pops, and I cast the offending foliage to the side as I reach for a clump of ferns. My claws tear through the delicate fronds, shredding them into green confetti. Throwing my head back, I let out a sound that's halfway between a shriek and a howl. In the distance, a dog starts to bark.

Now, more than ever, I want to die. I shouldn't have run away. I should have stood there, like the idiot I am, and just waited for the girl's father to come home. He would've put me out of my misery.

Well, he would have tried to, anyway.

Panting in frustration, I sink into a crouch and press my forehead against the rough bark of the tree, below the patchwork of score marks I've carved into it with my claws. I'm keenly aware of my tail lying on the ground behind me, of my wings trembling as I pull them forward as if to create a shield. Though my body has, over the years, disgusted me and scared me and caused me more physical pain than I care to think about, this is the first time it's actually embarrassed me. Now, it feels like the shame I should've felt all along has caught up with me. I want to rend this body limb from limb. I would, if I thought it would do anything other than just cause an afternoon of agony.

The snap of a twig makes me jump, and I spring to my feet, wings thrown wide. The girl takes a step back, looking more uncertain than fearful. Her ponytail is marginally tidier, and she's wearing clothes now with her boots, a pair of worn jeans and a waterproof jacket that's zipped all the way up to her neck. There's a chicken tucked under one arm, a plastic container in her other hand.

I narrow my eyes and take a step back. "What do you want?"

"I just wanted to check on you."

"Why?"

She frowns, like the answer should be obvious. "Because you were shot twice last night." I can practically feel her confused gaze as it sweeps over my shoulder and chest.

"I heal quickly."

"I can see that."

"I'm fine."

A skeptical eyebrow rises as she hitches the squirming bird up under her arm. "You're not hungry?"

I stare longingly at the chicken, then heave a huge sigh.

"I baked some muffins this morning," she says, holding out the plastic container. "Blueberry. They're really good."

That's the smell I detected around her earlier. I'm suddenly hit with a wave of memory: standing on a chair at the counter, putting the little paper muffin cups into the tin so Mom could pour the batter in. I shake my head and edge toward my discarded gloves, pushing the thought back where it belongs.

"No, thank you."

"Oh." Her hand falls. She looks down at the chicken. "I wasn't sure what you eat. I thought I'd offer, anyway." Taking a deep breath, she looks back up at me. "You wanted a chicken, didn't you?"

I say nothing as I pull the gloves back on, watching her face the whole time. She's struggling with something; I can see it in the way her expression flickers and changes, as if she makes up her mind, and then changes it, and then changes it again. Finally, she sighs, and the corners of her mouth quiver.

"You can have Linda," she says, looking down at the chicken tucked under her arm. "She's old, though, so I don't know if she'll taste very good."

"Linda?"

"Yeah. I named her after my nan."

Great. How am I supposed to eat a chicken named after her grandmother?

"She stopped laying a couple of weeks ago, and Dad says it's a waste of chicken feed to keep her around. I just couldn't . . . you know." She takes a step toward me. "Anyway, you can have her. I know you're hungry."

I hesitate. Is she really offering me one of her birds? Or is this a trick? I scan the trees behind her, searching for any sign of danger, someone lurking there with a gun, perhaps. But, as far as I can tell, we're alone.

"Thank you," I say, but I make no move to step forward and take the chicken. Sensing my hesitation, she gives me a quick, shy smile and bends over to set the plastic box of muffins on the ground. From her pocket, she pulls a piece of string, which she loops around one of Linda's ankles. She holds the other end, playing with the frayed bit between her fingers.

"Do you want me to . . . um . . . kill her for you?"

"No!" My sharp word startles her, and I can tell she wants to take a step back. "No, I like fresh meat."

"It *will* be fresh."

"I like live meat."

"Oh." She looks down at Linda, and another wave of shame washes over me. She bends down to tie the end of the string around a sapling, giving the feathers on the back of the chicken's neck a stroke when she's done. Then she picks up the box and holds it in front of her. "Are you sure you don't want a muffin?"

I kind of do. No, I *want* to want one. But I don't. The idea of chowing down on a blueberry muffin is about as appetizing as the thought of eating sawdust. I shake my head.

"Okay. Well. Enjoy your chicken, then." She stands there,

and she looks like she's trying not to cry. I feel like I might scream if she doesn't get out of here soon so I can eat. The sight of Linda straining on her string is making my mouth water again, and I can feel the saliva leaking out of my mouth, dribbling to the ground. Will today's string of embarrassments ever end?

To my great relief, after one last glance at the chicken, the girl slowly turns around and starts to pick her way through the trees. I watch her go, then pull off my gloves once more. Crouching, I prepare to leap toward the panicked fowl.

"Do you have a name?"

I freeze, looking up. The girl is stopped a few feet away, her fingers clutched around her muffin box. I nod slowly. "Sam."

"San?"

Stupid lipless mouth. I take a deep breath. "No. Sam."

"Sam?" When I nod, she smiles. "Like, short for Samuel?"

"Samson."

"Oh. I like that. It's a nice name. Maybe I'll use it for Linda's replacement."

"It's a boy's name."

She laughs and shakes her head. "Samantha, then." She tucks an escaped strand of hair behind her ear. "I'm Tegan."

"Tegan." To my great relief, my mutated mouth doesn't mangle her name. She smiles again as she turns away.

"Enjoy your chicken, Sam."

This time, I make sure she's out of view before turning my attention back to the bird. Linda squawks when I catch her up between my claws. I've never eaten anything this big before, but I'm not about to be picky. Unlike with my ratty meals, though, I go for the head first. Though it might be the best bit, and I'd prefer to save it for dessert, I don't want Tegan to hear Linda's last moments. So I bite off the bird's head and swallow it whole, grimacing as the beak scratches my throat. I wait until the rest of the chicken stops flailing before tearing into the gamey meat. It's not my preferred way of eating, but I'm not feeling particularly finicky at the moment.

As bite after bite of Linda the chicken accumulates in my stomach, I feel relief flood through me. I crouch over the remains of the carcass as I pluck out the long feathers so they don't get stuck in my teeth, and eat until the smell of chicken blood is no longer an agonizing tease for a starving monster, but just a reminder of a satisfying meal.

• 12 •

Why, Yes, I Am an Ass

Linda gives me a food coma, and I spend the afternoon sprawled on the forest floor, staring up into the treetops and letting the mist settle on my skin. My gloves lie abandoned a few feet away; I don't particularly want to put my messy hands back inside. I'm too embarrassed to ask Tegan for a wet cloth or some disinfecting wipes, though. I ate her chicken. A chicken that she *named*.

I might as well have eaten her kitten.

I think I'm probably not going to see her for a while, so I'm surprised when she turns up the next morning. After a quick glance at the empty string—the loose end of which is now a rusty brown—she turns her gaze on me. I'm crouched against the base of a tree, feeling a bit bloated from my massive meal the day before, but also stronger than I've felt in days.

"So? How was it?"

"How was what?"

"The chicken."

"Linda was delicious."

She blanches a little and stuffs her hands in her jacket pockets. "Not too gamey?"

I shrug. That was the first time I've ever eaten raw chicken. I don't really have anything to compare it to.

She takes a step closer, like a little kid testing her boundaries. I suspect she thinks I'll leap to my feet and charge her at any moment. I make a mental note to keep any sudden moves to a minimum.

"So . . . Dad's all excited about your visit the other night." She kicks at a pinecone with her boot. We both watch it bounce across the ground and come to rest near my foot. I pick it up and snap off some of the seeds.

"He tried to kill me."

"Yeah, well, he thought you were a monster."

I look up, startled at her words. "I am."

She shakes her head. "He's looking up all kinds of crazy stuff on the internet, trying to figure out what you are. His working theory is a chupacabra."

I snort hard, and the air whistles through my nostril slits. "I do not suck goats."

She shrugs. "I didn't think so. I mean, you left ours alone and went straight for the chickens."

"You have goats?"

"Yeah, in the barn. Why? You want one?"

She's just teasing me. The twinkle in her eye gives her away. Still, I consider the idea. A goat might be tasty. But if Linda was almost more than I could handle, then a goat surely would be. And I wouldn't want to waste all that meat.

Without waiting for my answer, she walks even closer and kneels down on the damp ground. She's only a few feet away, staring at me with wide eyes.

"It's rude to stare."

"Sorry. It's just . . . I had no idea anything like you even existed. And then to find out you can talk! Omigod. If Dad knew I was actually having a conversation with you, he'd flip."

I'm sure he would.

"So. Sam." She smiles as she says my name, as if she can't quite believe she's sitting here, having this conversation. To be honest, I can't quite believe it, either. "Where are you from?"

I blink and remain silent.

"Do you live with your family? Others like you?"

"No."

"How old are you?"

I sigh through my nostrils. "Seventeen."

"Really?" Her gaze takes all of me in, lingering a little too long on the area between my bent legs. "I haven't seen you at school."

"I don't go to school."

"I know, Sam. Obviously." She shakes her head.

"Why are you talking to me?"

The question seems to bring her up short. She rubs her palms over the knees of her jeans and looks at the ground. "I don't know. I thought . . . I thought you might want someone to talk to. I thought you might be lonely."

"I'm not lonely." My voice sounds petulant. I toss the mangled pinecone into the brush.

"Sorry. My mistake. I guess all your friends are out of town for the weekend."

I stand abruptly, ignoring my earlier resolution to avoid any sudden moves. My teeth click in agitation, and she looks up, her gaze snagging on my naked front, which is just about at her eye level. "Go away," I growl.

"Um, excuse me." She stands up and brushes the debris from her soaked knees. "This is *our* property. If anyone should go away, it's you."

"Fine." I turn and start to storm away, scooping up my gloves from the ground as I go.

"Sam, wait."

"What?"

"I'm sorry. Please, don't go."

I stop, my breath hitching in my chest. "Why not?"

"Just . . . I don't know. I'm being rude, and I'm sorry. Stay. Please. Talk to me."

I turn around slowly. She stands there, looking a little lost. Her dark brown eyes are wide, pleading, as if I'm her best friend about to run away forever. "Are *you* lonely?" I ask.

"At the moment, yes." She sighs and puts her hands back in her pockets. "You get kind of left out of things when you live so far from town. And it doesn't help when your dad's got a reputation for being a little . . . obsessed about certain things."

"What things?"

"Whatever he's thinking about at the moment. Right now, it's monsters in the woods."

"What about your mother?" I know that lots of girls count their mother as their best friend. So I'm pretty sure I already know the answer she's going to give me.

"She died when I was six."

"I'm sorry."

"Yeah." She sighs. "Me, too." Her head tilts to the side as she considers me. "What about you? I know you said you don't live with your parents, but—"

"My father's alive." At least, I think he is. He hasn't bothered to contact me in over a decade, but I haven't seen any notice of his death in the obituaries. And, believe me, I've been checking.

"But not your mom."

I shake my head.

"Well, we have something in common, then."

"Not really." I'm pretty sure Tegan didn't kill her own mother with a set of poison claws. She ignores my last comment and moves toward me again. I take a wary step back, aware of my exposed hands.

"So what's with those things?"

"What things?"

"On your back." She holds her arms out to the sides and waves them up and down. I can't tell if she's mocking me or not.

"They're called wings."

"Wings are usually for flying. And I have yet to see you fly."

I shrug.

"Have you ever tried?"

"Of course."

"And?"

"It didn't work."

"So did you try again?"

My teeth click in agitation. My fingers twitch. I really

should put my gloves back on. The thought of nicking her with a claw to shut her up is all too tempting.

"If I had wings," she goes on, seemingly oblivious to my distress, "you'd better believe I'd be out there practising every day. Who wouldn't want to fly?"

"Penguins."

"Sam, those are not penguin wings."

I pull them tightly against my back, trying to make them as small as possible. She grins.

"Nice try. Come on. Unfurl those bad boys and let's see what they can do."

I gape at her in disbelief.

"Sam, just try."

"No."

She eyes the tree behind me and points up into the branches. "Go on. Get up there and jump. Trial by fire, right? Or we could always find a nice cliff, and I could push you off."

My teeth are clicking and I can't make them stop. Who does she think she is? They're *my* wings, and I already know they don't work. Why won't she listen?

"Sam, come on."

"If I do, will you stop pestering me about it?"

Her face breaks out in a massive grin. "Yes."

I toss the gloves to the ground at the base of the tree and grab the trunk. I manage to shimmy up the first few feet, keeping my knees locked tightly around the rough bark. Digging my claws in, I pull myself up, inch by inch. I'm getting scratches and scrapes where I never wanted them, and I know that, in a few minutes, I'm in for even more pain. But it'll shut her up, so it will be worth it.

I reach the first branch about fifteen feet up and hook my leg over it, swinging myself up to straddle the limb. When I look down, Tegan has her head tilted back, her hand shading her eyes, even though there's not much sunlight to speak of in here.

"Don't be afraid," she calls up to me.

"I'm not." I look up, spying the next branch about four feet above my head. If I'm going to do this, I might as well make it spectacular.

"Sam, what are you doing? You're high enough."

I ignore her as I climb up to the next branch. And then the next. And the one after that. As I plant my feet on the thick limb and curl my toes around it, I dare a glance down. I'm probably up too high, and even if I *were* able to fly, there are a couple of branches below me that would be in the way. But it's not about flying. It's about showing her that she doesn't know anything about me, even if she thinks she does.

"Sam? You're too high."

"You're the one who thinks I can fly. What are you worried about?"

"If you fall, you're going to hurt yourself."

"Of course I am." Sidestepping carefully away from the trunk, I unfurl my wings and spread them wide, stretching the muscles and tendons until my shoulders ache. I crouch down in preparation, wobbling a little as I try to keep my balance. Tegan lets out a squeak that's audible all the way up on my perch.

"Sam. *Sam!*"

Her voice climbs into a scream as I launch myself out into the air. Gravity snatches me, and my outward arc curves down as I'm sucked toward the ground. My wings give a feeble flap, my descent slows, and, for just a moment, I wonder if maybe she was right, that I can fly after all.

That lasts for about three seconds. I twist at the last moment, and my right wing buckles under me as I slam into the ground, the delicate bones that hold the membrane snapping. The pain isn't quite what it was when I ripped my wings from my own body a few days ago, but it's bad enough. My breath comes in short, sharp bursts of sound that do little to warn off the girl who throws herself toward me.

"Stay back!" I shout as I curl my hands into tight fists in an effort to keep the claws hidden.

"Are you all right? No, Sam, you're not," she says, answering her own question. She takes a step toward me and reaches for my arm.

"Stay *back!*" The second word comes out in a shriek that sets my own teeth on edge. "Go away! I told you, I can't fly."

"Then why did you try?"

"To shut you up." I roll onto my front and push myself onto my hands and knees, making sure nothing touches either of my wings. The right one is throbbing, and I can feel something trickling along the membrane.

"Omigod, Sam. You're bleeding. Do you need—"

"I need you to get the hell away from me." I stand up. "I need you to grow a brain and think about what you're doing. Do you realize how easily I could kill you? Do you ever think about your own safety? Look at me. Do I look like an appropriate friend for a teenage girl?" I've rarely strung so many words together since the transformation, and I know half of them don't sound right. But Tegan just stands

there, staring at me in disbelief, and I realize that, somehow, she's understood every word.

"Ass."

"What?"

"You heard me, Sam. You're an ass."

"And you're a pushy know-it-all who's about to get eaten."
She blinks. "Really?"

I can't help it. Her completely inadequate reaction strikes right in the middle of my long-dormant sense of humour. The laugh bursts from between my teeth before I can stop it. It sounds so strange, rusty and underused. I clamp my teeth together, and the chuckle continues to whistle through my nostril slits. Tegan looks half amused, half insulted, and completely unsure about whether to laugh or snark at me some more.

"No more flying practice," I say when the chuckle has played itself out. She nods solemnly.

"No. Not today, anyway."

I shoot her a dark look and click my teeth at her, but she's so busy fretting over the state of my wing that she doesn't notice.

"Are you going to be okay?"

"Yes. I heal fast, remember?"

She narrows her eyes. "You could have reminded me before I freaked out."

I turn and take a good look at my wing. The bone that snapped in two is already healing, albeit crookedly. I sigh and flick a drop of blood from the membrane with the back of my finger. "Where's the fun in that?"

"Ass."

I click my teeth in her direction once more, but all she does is smile.

• 13 •

A Curse of Eggs and Rodents

I don't see her again for a couple of days, which is just as well. She seems to either piss me off (which makes me want to kill her) or laugh (causing a reflex that makes me want to kill myself).

During the day, I try to stay hidden, but it's not that easy, especially now with the colder weather stripping the leaves from the trees and bushes. What was once green and alive turns brown and brittle, and soon even the sound of my passage through the trees seems so loud that I'm sure I'll be discovered at any moment. After the sun goes down, I prowl to the edge of the woods, but I'm not brave enough to venture any farther than that, since it would require crossing a road and being out in the open.

When she returns near sunset on the third day, she's out of breath, like she ran all the way. Her hair is loose, and the skirt she's wearing gives me a nice view of her shapely legs. I try not to stare, but I don't have much luck.

"I'm sorry. I couldn't get away before. Dad'll be home from work in a few minutes, and if I'm not there when he walks in the door, he'll get all paranoid. Did you know there are monsters in the woods?"

"So I've heard."

She gives a short laugh and carefully pulls something from her pocket and holds it out to me. It's an egg, light brown and faintly speckled.

"I thought you might be hungry. I know you haven't eaten any more chickens. Not ours, anyway. Have you found some squirrels or something? I know there are a few around. I've heard them."

I blink dumbly.

"Do you eat eggs?" she asks, suddenly sounding unsure.

The truth is, I've never really tried. The thought isn't completely abhorrent, though, which means my body will probably be okay with it. I nod.

"Oh, good." She lets out a sigh of relief as she continues to hold the egg out to me. "I can get you some more, too. Later, though." She looks back toward the house nervously. I take the opportunity to pluck the egg from her outstretched hand with my gloved fingers. She jumps, and stares at the empty space where the egg used to be.

"Thank you."

"You're welcome, Sam. I know it's not much, especially if you're used to . . . you know . . . meat."

"It's okay. I know chickens don't grow on trees."

She laughs, then claps her hand over her mouth. My tingling nether regions are grateful for that.

"I gotta go," she whispers, turning away. "I'll try to come back soon. Will you be here tonight?"

I don't want her to get into trouble with her father, so I don't respond. She doesn't wait for a response, anyway. I know I'm going to get a visit tonight, whether I like it or not.

My tail shuffles against the dead leaves as I crouch and contemplate the egg. Like chicken (until recently, anyway), eggs are something I've never eaten raw. I used to like them scrambled, with so much pepper they made me sneeze. That doesn't seem too appealing now. But I'm not quite sure how to go about eating this one. I'm pretty good at swallowing rat heads, and Linda's noggin went down without too much of a problem, but the egg is bigger than either, and I really don't want to choke to death out here. Mind you, then I guess Tegan's father would get to have his little bonfire after all.

Finally, I decide to just go for it. I toss it into the air, like I've seen people in movies do with popcorn, and catch it in my mouth. My teeth crunch through the shell as if it's nothing. I tilt my head back and let the gooey innards slide down my throat. The shell bits grind between my teeth as I work through them. I carefully lick the shards from my fangs and swallow as much as I can.

Not bad. It's going to take more than one egg to make a meal, but it's a start. I hate having to depend on Tegan for this, but it's really no different than it was in the hospital. I've always been dependent on others for my food, even though I look like I should be able to hunt for myself.

I spend the next few hours fashioning a sort of nest, gathering dead leaves and piling them in a depression formed by the roots of a tall tree. When Tegan finds me there, crouching in the crunchy leaves, my wings tucked close against my back, she bursts out laughing.

"You look like a chicken." The beam of her flashlight sweeps over me, and I click my teeth in annoyance. "A very weird chicken."

I let out a chirp, which startles her. The subsequent chuckle whistles through my nostrils.

"I brought a couple more eggs," she says, and I can see that she does indeed have two more elongated orbs clutched between the fingers of the hand that's not holding the flashlight. "How was the last one?"

"Good."

"That was from Fifi. She's one of my best layers. These two are from Helga and Stevie. They should be just as good, even though Dad says Stevie's eggs should be sour, on account of her temperament. She's kind of a bitch." She turns the back of her hand toward me, and I can see a faint red line. "And she wasn't happy about sharing with you."

"Maybe I should eat her."

"Maybe. When she's stopped giving us eggs." She steps closer to my nest. I cup my gloved hands and she gently places the eggs into them. Then, to my horror, she plunks herself down on the ground, less than a foot away. I edge sideways, and my tail catches at the dead leaves, scattering a few of them. "So," she says, letting the word hang in the air as if it's supposed to magically start a conversation all on its own. My stomach lets out a growl. It's aware of the proximity of the eggs and is wondering why they're not coming down the hatch already. "Go ahead and eat," Tegan says as she uses the end of the flashlight to dig a little divot in the dirt. She places the flashlight into the hole and pats the loose dirt into place, propping it up so the beam shines into the sky. I'm still mostly in shadow, but I really don't want her to be around when I try to eat these eggs.

"I have bad table manners."

"Do your kind usually eat at tables?"

"No."

"Well, then, the fact that you have *any* table manners is pretty impressive."

Screw it. Maybe if she sees me eat, she'll get grossed out enough that she'll leave me alone. I crunch into one of the eggs, slurping as loudly as I can. Some of the egg white drips down onto my knee, and I lick it away with an exaggerated swipe of my tongue. When I'm done, I look up to meet her gaze, challenging.

"So, aside from chickens and eggs, what do you usually eat?"

For crying out loud. I slam the other egg into my mouth, crunch the shell as if to show her how I could snap through her bones with my teeth if I wanted to, and swallow loudly before answering. "Teenage girls."

"Yeah, right. You're full of it, Sam."

With a growl, I turn away and rest the underside of my jaw on my knee.

"Cows?" When I say nothing, she continues. "Sheep? Horses? Dogs? Cats? Oh, wait, I know. Fish. Do you eat fish?"

"No."

"Sam, come on."

"Rats."

"Rats?" She's so close I can feel her shudder. "Well, I guess protein is protein . . ." Out of the corner of my eye, I see the light flicker. I look up. She's waving her hand through the beam, causing leaning shadows to flicker around her fingers. Her perfect, human fingers with the right number of knuckles and ten achingly normal fingernails covered in chipped green polish.

"Tegan," I say, and the sound of her name makes her pause, her hand spread above the flashlight's little bulb. "What's the date?"

"The date? Um . . . October fourteenth, I think. Why?" She leans closer, as if she's going to nudge me with her elbow. But she doesn't quite touch me. "Do you have someplace you need to be?"

My birthday—and the curse's completion—is a little over two weeks away. I know my mind is treading into dangerous territory. Hopeful territory. I can't let that happen. I need to be realistic. For all I know, my memory—clouded by a seven-year-old boy's terror and pain—is mistaken. Dr. Grant might be right. The transformation was probably some weird medical condition. Unusual, yes . . . but possibly able to be explained by science. Just because I've never heard of another case like mine doesn't mean they aren't out there. After all, Dr. Grant kept me a secret for almost eleven years; who's to say other doctors aren't doing the same thing with their own monstrous patients?

And even if it is a curse that *can* be broken . . . well, I'm out of luck there, too. Because as friendly and as curious as

Tegan is, I know that's all she is. And that's all she should be. If she were somehow able to fall in love with a monster like me, I would be quite concerned about her mental well-being.

"Sam?"

I realize I haven't said anything for far too long. With a whistling sigh, I turn my head away again. "It's my birthday."

"When?"

"October thirty-first."

"Omigod." She giggles, then catches herself. "I'm sorry, Sam. It's just . . . Halloween? That's, like, weirdly appropriate, isn't it?"

"Why?"

"Because you're . . . um . . ." She trails off, and I can feel her unease now. She knows she's stepped in it. And I'm not about to let her off the hook.

"I'm what?"

"You're . . . you."

"I'm what?" I say again, my voice deepening into a growl. I watch her out of the corner of my eye. She looks like she's about to cry. Good.

"Sam, I'm sorry. I didn't mean . . ." She lunges for the flashlight and picks it up, swinging the beam away and plunging me into darkness. I blink as my eyes struggle to adjust. "Do you want me to bring you some more eggs tomorrow?"

"No."

"Sam . . ."

I can hear the misery in her voice now. I stand slowly, my wings trembling against my back. I want to run, but I have nowhere to go. Instead, I do the thing I know will hurt her the most. I turn my back on her and settle myself on the ground.

"Sam, please. I'm sorry." Her voice is plaintive. I try to ignore her. "Talk to me. Please."

I clench my jaw and remain silent. The beam of the flashlight hits the tree beside me, then disappears. I hear her footsteps retreat. Almost hidden under the whispering crunch of leaves is the soft sound of her sniffling.

I want to feel good about making her cry. A monster would. But, somehow, I'm not there yet.

I guess I have a couple more weeks of humanity left in me before it's gone for good.

• 14 •

Don't Blow It, Sam

When she appears the next day in the fading after-noon, her eyes are bloodshot. I pause from my nest tidying.

"You look tired," I say.

"Yeah, well, I didn't sleep." Her hands are shoved deep in her jacket pockets, her fists straining hard against the material. "I just . . . I just wanted to apologize for—"

"You didn't do anything."

"Sam, I did. And I—"

"Never mind." I straighten up and look down at my nest. It's bigger than the previous version. Despite my best efforts to stay curled and small, I ended up sprawled on my back and woke with the leaves scat-tered uselessly around my crushed wings. "Does this look comfortable?"

"Not really." She shrugs, staring at the ground. "But

maybe it is. I don't know. I mean, maybe it is . . . for your kind." Her lip wavers precariously. I sigh.

"You're right. It doesn't look comfortable." I roll my shoulders for emphasis, then let them sag. "I miss my old bed."

"Your bed?"

I'm sure she's thinking of something really rustic, padded with moss and leaves, perhaps decorated with feathers. I'm almost tempted to tell her it was a metal frame with an actual mattress and sheets, but that would open myself up to so many questions. So I just nod and say, "It was comfortable."

Abandoning the pathetic nest of dead leaves, I walk a couple of steps and lower myself to the ground. Tegan still looks so unsure, and the expression seems unnatural on her. It's weirding me out. I wish I could give her an encouraging smile to let her know I'm not holding what she said yesterday against her.

Not that the girl needs much encouraging.

Besides, she was right. I know I look like something you'd buy at a cheap party-supply store to prop up in the corner of your porch on Halloween. I'm not stupid.

"Is your wing all healed now?"

"It's fine." I hold it out to the side to show her. It did heal crooked, and now it won't spread out quite as far as the other one. She winces.

"Does it hurt? It looks . . . painful."

"No." I shake it a little, sending the membrane flapping. "If I ever do learn to fly, though, I'll probably go around in circles."

Her face crumples for a moment, but then breaks into a

tentative smile as she realizes I'm joking. "I'm sorry I made you fall."

"You didn't. You were trying to get me to fly." I fold my wing next to the other one against my back. "I'm the one who jumped out of a tree."

"So . . . you're a reckless idiot, like most of the boys at school."

"I *am* seventeen."

"Do you also drive too fast?"

I shake my head. "I don't drive at all. My wings get caught on the seatbelt."

She laughs and steps toward me, and my heart picks up its pace. I watch as she pauses and then sits down, folding herself onto the ground. Her knee is only inches from my own. I don't move, though. I'm almost afraid to.

Like she's done before, she studies me carefully. But, this time, I don't feel her gaze as intrusive. There's no judgment, only simple curiosity. I glance down at her hand resting on her leg. Though her skin is not exactly fair, next to my dark-grey flesh, it's quite a contrast. When I turn my gaze up to her face, I'm struck by the humanness of her pretty, dark-brown eyes. Even bloodshot, they're lovely. Her lashes sweep down, then back up, and with the movement comes a shy smile. I take a deep breath.

"Do you think I'm ugly?"

She studies me for a moment, her gaze lingering on my exposed teeth. "That's not for me to judge, Sam. I mean, you could be, like, a supermodel among your kind."

"Do *you* think I'm ugly?"

"Well, you're not the sort of guy I usually find attrac—"

My huge sigh cuts her off, and she throws up her hands.

"What do you want me to say? That you're so hideous I can't even bear to look at you?"

"That's the truth."

"No. It isn't." As she says this, she's looking right at me, her gaze unflinching. Somehow, I believe she's telling the truth. Or . . . she thinks she is.

I don't understand her at all.

A moment later, a tentative finger joins her gaze in exploring my face. I go still, afraid to move, worrying about her delicate skin so close to my teeth. But she keeps her hand well away from my mouth. I can feel her touch on my cheekbone, then my brow. I hold my breath as it moves around the side of my head to my earhole.

"Your skin is softer than it looks," she says. I say nothing, but let my breath out slowly. We both hear it whistle through the slits of my nostrils. Abandoning my head, she lets her fingers trail down my arm before finally breaking contact. "What's with the gloves?"

"What?"

"The gloves, Sam." She points to my hands. I curl my fingers into fists and rest them in my lap. "You don't wear a stitch of clothing, but you've got these beautiful gloves on your hands. Why?"

"Claws."

"Really?" Her eyes widen, but it's not an expression of horror. She's just curious. I'm beginning to think her curiosity has no limit. "Your toes have claws," she points out, "and I don't see you wearing socks."

I shrug. The poison issue really isn't something I feel like getting into. She already thinks I'm some sort of oddity; I'm afraid if she finds out I have fatal fingernails, she might actually squeal with excitement.

"Can I see?"

"What?"

"Your fingers, Sam. Can I see them?"

I sigh again. Why not? Slowly, carefully, I start to pull the glove from my right hand. "Don't touch," I say as I see her shuffle a couple of inches closer on her knees.

"I won't."

I pull the glove off and flex my fingers a few times so she can get a good look. The extra knuckle is something I'm used to now, but she obviously isn't expecting it. She sucks in a little gasp and looks up at my face.

"You must have great dexterity."

"Not really."

An amused smile spreads across her features, and she goes back to studying my hand. I turn it over, palm side up, so she can see the undersides of my claws. Shiny and black, they're as sharp as needles, and although Dr. Grant had the gloves made to protect those around me, I'm actually pretty grateful for them myself. Even though any cuts I might inflict on my own body heal almost immediately, they can still be painful.

"That's quite the manicure," she says.

"I've never had a manicure." That's not quite true. One of the nurses tried to trim the claws during the first few weeks I was at the hospital. They grew back as sharp as ever by the time I went to bed that night.

"Too bad. They'd probably look awesome painted gold."

I give her a blank stare.

"I'm kidding, Sam." She shakes her head with a smile. For a few moments, she's quiet as she stares thoughtfully into the trees. Aside from the rustle of wind in the leaves, I can't hear much else. The other forest creatures are still keeping their distance. That's probably wise of them.

Tegan suddenly turns back to me, and by the look on her face I know I'm about to be hit with another question.

"What do your kind look like as children?"

I jerk as if she's struck me, and my teeth click in surprise. What am I supposed to tell her? That I didn't always look like this? That I once had skin like hers, glowing with vitality, delicately flecked with sun-gifted freckles? Green eyes that sparkled with life? Little white teeth that wiggled and fell out and were exchanged for money under the pillow? I pull my knees to my chest and wrap my arms around them. My wings tremble, as if they long to curl around me, to shelter me from her questions. I need to say something; she's waiting for my answer. "I don't know."

"Sam, you must know. What did you look like when you were younger?"

"The same. But smaller." It isn't a lie. But she doesn't look like she believes me. Or maybe she's just not satisfied with my answer. She sits on her heels and goes back to studying me.

"Did you have wings then?"

"Yes."

"And your teeth . . ."

I nod. My teeth changed along with the rest of me. They were smaller, of course, and continued to fall out and be replaced, as baby teeth do. When the black fangs fell out at the age of ten, I prayed to anyone who would listen that they wouldn't grow back. But of course they did, longer and sharper than before.

"And your skin—"

I'm so caught up in the old memory of those early years that I don't realize her fingers are drifting toward my wrist until I feel her touch. Overriding the instinct to pull away, I look down to see her tender skin just inches from my deadly claws. My breaths turn into pants, and my teeth click together in agitation. "Don't touch."

"Sam, it's not that bad. If you would just—"

"Don't *touch!*"

The guttural shout seems to startle her, and she pulls her hand back. Relief floods through me as I realize disaster has been averted, but the anger remains. I tug the glove back over my fingers and unfold myself from the ground. She looks up at me, her eyes wide. I've frightened her, but she's trying not to let it show.

"I'm sorry, Sam. I won't . . . I won't touch you." She gets to her feet, and though I can see her hands shaking, she doesn't turn away. I breathe heavily, pushing the whistling air through my nostrils.

"I don't want you to feel sorry for me," I growl. Her eyes flash as she folds her arms across her chest.

"I didn't say I was. I said I was sorry for touching—" She breaks off as I shake out my wings and spread them wide. I advance toward her, my shoulders curled low like an animal ready to spring.

"I don't need your pity."

"Sam . . ." Her voice is a whimper now, her eyes frightened

as she backs away from me. Her feet stumble as she trips over a root and falls back on a tree. She flattens herself against it while I step up close.

Why am I trying to scare her? All I want to do is cry, but the curse has ensured that's something I'll never do again. The grief and rage inside me has no other outlet, and it builds until it feels like it might claw its way out, leaving my skin in shreds.

Tegan turns her head away and closes her eyes, as if the sight of me is too much to bear. I know she was lying before. She had to be. Nobody can look at my face and not feel horror at what they see.

"Do you pity me?" The words almost catch in my throat, and my teeth click of their own accord. She presses her lips together and keeps her head turned away. "Answer me!"

"Yes. Yes, I pity you, Sam. I pity someone who hurts other people, because they only do that if they've been hurt themselves."

I want to tell her she knows nothing about me. I want to tell her she doesn't know what she's talking about.

But she's right. And it makes me furious.

The shriek builds in my chest and erupts out of me, causing my whole body to quake like it's going to tear apart. I open my mouth wide, letting the sound build until its screeching grates against my ears. In the distance, dogs begin to bark and howl, as if trying to answer. But there is no answer to what I'm feeling. What normal creature could possibly understand what I'm feeling?

I snap my jaw shut and back up from Tegan. She keeps her eyes closed, her head turned away. Any hope I might have had—that I might have stupidly let myself feel—is gone, and when I see her trembling, I know it's something I'll never have again. The strange urge to apologize forces my mouth open once more, but I clamp down on the feeling. I am a monster. Monsters don't apologize.

I turn away and fold my wings tightly against my back.

"Sam . . ."

Without waiting, without turning to see the fear in her eyes, I bolt into the trees, away from her. Away from her questions. Away from my memories of what once was. Of what was lost. Of what will never be again. I run as the sun dips toward the horizon and the trees fall into shadow.

And then I'm just another shadow among them, a creature of the night, hidden away for the good of everyone.

• 15 •

You Blew It, Sam

I want to go home. Everything's a mess. I've made everything a mess. I just want to go back to the way things were.
I want to go back to my windowless room, my comfortable
bed, my daily rat and disinfecting wipes. I want to go back
to hiding. I don't want people to look at me anymore. I don't
want to see that fear in their eyes.

I tear across the blissfully empty road and into the field on
the other side, leaping over the fence and crouching low as I
run through the weeds. My goal is the stand of trees I can
see on the far end of the property. Actually, it looks more like
a proper forest. I can't see any breaks. The land rises up into a
ridge that runs along the horizon in front of me, covered by
the beckoning darkness of the trees. I narrow my focus and
hurtle forward. From the property to my left, as if they can
sense my presence, a couple of dogs begin to whine and bark.
I'm concentrating too hard on my mad dash to answer them.

The land is dark by the time I push my way into the trees. I don't know if anybody saw me slipping through the fields, but I haven't caught a glimpse of any torch-wielding farmers with pitchforks, so I'm probably okay. I continue to run until I can't see well enough to do so anymore, and I slide down a short embankment, stumbling into a shallow creek. Breathing hard, I stop, swaying on my feet. All I can hear is the whistle of air through my nostrils and the slight trickle of the water that runs over my toes.

When my skin has absorbed its fill and it feels like I'm wearing a pair of cushy slippers (or what I imagine slippers must feel like, because I've never actually worn any), I venture back out into the trees bordering the creek. I shake out my wings and sink down against a tree, pressing my knobbly humped back against the bark.

I'm totally screwed. As if to underscore that point, my stomach begins to growl. I tear the glove from my right hand and rake my claws over my stomach. They snag and catch, tearing the flesh with an audible noise.

"Shut up!" I scream. As if my stomach will somehow become chastened and start to behave itself.

I'm yelling at a sac of acid. I'm losing it.

The way I see it, I have two choices. I can try to make my way back to the hospital—somehow—and get Dr. Grant to take me back. The last part shouldn't be that hard; it's the first part that I can't figure out how to do. Then there's the second option, which is to figure out how to feed myself and make a new life out here. A life where I don't have to be someone's science project or object of pity.

You can probably sense which way I'm leaning.

It's too bad I'm not actually nocturnal, despite my affinity with the darkness. My night vision just isn't good enough, and I do tend to sleep better at night than during the day. The last couple of weeks notwithstanding, of course.

So. Tomorrow I will make a concerted effort to find myself something to eat. I don't care if it scurries or flies or walks on two legs. Okay, maybe that's just the hunger talking. Despite my annoyance with some humans I've met recently, I'm not quite ready to eat any of them.

Yet.

I pull my glove back on, noticing the funky smell that wafts out as I push my fingers inside. I never should have put them back on my dirty hands, but what was I supposed to do? Ask Tegan if I could use their sink?

With a sigh, I tilt my head back until it rests against the tree, and close my eyes to the dark forest.

The sound of the creek makes me have to pee immediately upon opening my eyes the next morning. I relieve myself against the side of a tree, watching as the moss shrivels and peels away from the bark. I wonder if that's what usually happens, or if I've got poison piss as well as claws of catastrophe. I don't remember Dr. Grant mentioning anything about my urine tests, but then, he never really got into the specifics of my lab results with me.

I decide to take a walk. I follow the creek for a while, which twists and turns through the forest, diving under a fallen log, only to emerge on the other side like a river passing under a bridge. The light is definitely brighter off to my left, and I know that's probably where the fields are. I stay well back from the tree line, hoping the forest is far enough from any of the farmhouses that my dark form won't be seen.

My first hunting trip—if you can call it that—takes place at sundown. I slink through the grass, almost on my belly, keeping my wings tightly furled. A white cat spots me as I lurch toward the henhouse, but unlike the grey one I encountered on my first day of freedom, this one bolts without taking a stand. I have to admire its common sense.

The henhouse is dusty and stinks to high heaven. But after I close the door behind me, it's easy pickings. The birds squawk and scream as I plunge into their midst. I'm like a wild animal that's never been taught to hunt by its mother.

In other words, I'm absolutely terrible at it.

The first bird escapes, leaving me with a handful of feathers, one of which gets stuck on a claw. I don't even bother to pull it off before making my second attempt. This time, I get a better grip. I fall on the bird, nearly crushing it with my body. As it tries to escape, wings flapping in panic, I sink my teeth into its side. One wing comes off in my mouth, and downy feathers tickle my tongue. I chomp down hard, breaking the bones so I can swallow the flesh. The second bite tears further into the chicken, and blood pours into my mouth as my fangs rip some major artery. The rest of the chickens have pressed themselves into a far corner, flapping and clucking and nearly climbing each other in their desire to escape. But they don't need to worry. My eyes aren't bigger than my stomach.

I finish the bird, crouching by the door. The head goes in last, but it's not quite as good as I expect. A twinge of something—either remorse or disgust—floods through me in a burst as I survey the floor, now covered in feathers, chicken crap, and blood. My stomach aches with satiety, and I push the twinge away. I open the door and slip out into the darkening night.

I awake the next morning to find bits of feather and down stuck to the dried blood on my chest. The water from the creek solves the problem quickly, and I spend a little longer than usual in the flow, rubbing the cold water over my limbs, splashing it on my wings, shaking the droplets free like a giant bird in a birdbath. I let out a chirp of satisfaction and plunge my jaws into the water, using one claw to work free the bits of feather that have gotten stuck between my teeth. There really is nothing like a good meal and a bath, especially when you've gone for so long without. Standing, I shake my body free of water, then flap my wings hard. I close my eyes as the cool spray tickles my face.

Then I find myself a sunlit clearing between a stand of cedars, spread my limbs out on the ground, and doze while I thank the nameless chicken that has filled me with an almost indescribable sense of contentment.

• 16 •

Playing Chicken with Karma

Two days later, I venture farther afield. My gloves lie abandoned by the creek. I don't need them anymore; in fact, they'll only get in the way. I need my claws to pry open latches, to snag chickens, to hold them in place while they struggle in their pathetic death throes. They're so easy to catch now. They're predictable and easy to herd. Once they're all rustling together in a corner, it's just a matter of reaching in and grabbing the plumpest one.

The second farm only has two hens and a rooster, so I have to push away the twinge of guilt that snaps at me when I tear the wings off the rooster and swallow them nearly whole. The bones scratch and tear at my throat, but it's worth the discomfort. Now that I know what a full stomach—a *real* full stomach, not just a half-full-of-rat stomach—feels like, I can't imagine how I ever went as long as I did without these clucking balls of goodness. And I don't have to. The people around here are complacent. Sure, they've taken measures against foxes and raccoons and whatever else roams the woods around these parts, but they've neglected to think about creatures that are smart enough to undo complex latches and locks that require multiple steps and hand motions.

Lucky for me.

Unlucky for me, the rooster gets its revenge by giving me terrible gas. I spend the evening crouched next to the creek, listening to the rumbling of my guts as I moan in concert with them, all the while emitting terrible smells from my backside. The rooster was a bit tough and kind of gamey, and not worth the stinky anguish at all. I make a mental note to stick to hens in the future.

I give my innards a day to recover before heading back out. It seems that, the more I eat, the hungrier I get. It's almost inconceivable that I ever went so many days without eating anything at all, like I did immediately after my escape from the hospital. The hunger that drives me now is insistent and loud, an almost audible force screeching in my head. I give in to it and dive through the trees, heading in the opposite direction. It's time to scope out some new dining establishments.

As I approach the unfamiliar buildings through the weedy, unkempt fields, I sense that something's off. The air is . . . empty. As I near the falling-down barn, I spy the wooden coop on the other side of the fenced-in yard. The twilight shadows are still. I pop my head up from the weeds and take a good, long sniff. The whistle of air entering my nostrils sounds forlorn. Maybe that's just because I can't detect anything in it. No chickens. No feathers. Not even chicken poop. There haven't been any birds here for a while. I sink back down into the weeds with a rustle and a sigh.

The rustling continues, forming a swaying mass that cleaves through the weeds to my right. I brace my feet under me and slowly stand, keeping my body in a low crouch. The rustling stops, only to be replaced by a rumbling growl. I blink, staring into the shadows a few feet away. When I see what it is, my jaws pull open and my wings spread, like some kind of defence mechanism I didn't even know I had.

The dog's head is huge and square. Even its jaw is blocky. It's also full of sharp, white teeth that I can see past its pulled-back lips. It takes a deep breath and growls again. I lower my head and growl right back, then snap my teeth at it. The dog barks once, spit flying, and launches itself at me.

Perhaps I'm so stunned by the stupidity of the creature that it takes a moment before I can react. Then all I do is stumble backward and trip over my own feet, landing with a thud on my back. The dog pounces onto me, planting one of its front paws on my chest as its jaws aim straight for my throat. I throw up my right arm at the last moment, only to hear a crunch as the creature's powerful jaws clamp around it. It shakes hard, and the force of the wild movement terrifies me.

If it gets its teeth around something vital, I'm a goner.

Holding my arm away from myself as much as I can, I try to pull myself out from under the dog. It shakes my arm again, and the violent jerk tugs painfully on my shoulder. Letting out a growl, I snap my teeth at the dog, as if I'm going to bite it. But it doesn't believe me. Or it doesn't care. Its grip tightens, and I watch in horror as blood—my blood—gushes out around its teeth.

I bring my free hand back and punch hard, striking the dog in the side of the head. Nothing. I try again, this time aiming my blow at the dog's nose. The grip loosens for just a fraction of a second. I wrench my trapped arm, and it comes away. But I don't have time to celebrate. The dog lunges for me again. I twist and scramble, trying to push myself up to a standing position as I throw myself away from my attacker.

My scream rends the air as the dog grabs my right wing and pulls. I tumble onto the ground, and the next thing I see is the dog's face again, coming right for my throat. I let out a shriek of terror, and the dog suddenly comes up short, as if a spell has been broken. It looks around for a moment, its head swinging from side to side. I don't move. My wings lie crushed under me, and the fiery pain in the right one feels both hot and cold at the same time. Hissing breaths escape from between my teeth. The dog whines once and takes a step back.

I sit up, so slowly that it drags out the pain and almost makes me scream again, but the last thing I want to do is trigger the dog. It stares at me with an expression of cold stupidity. One of its eyes is light blue.

I edge sideways, crab-like, trying to fold my wings against my back as I do so. The dog watches me, its sides heaving. Its muzzle is smeared with red. I brace my feet under me, keeping my left hand pressed against the ground. A spark of something—a challenge, perhaps, or a warning—snaps through the air between us.

The dog lunges again.

I turn and run, back toward the woods, even though I know I can't outrun a dog. Especially not one this big. I've gone maybe six paces when there's a sharp piercing sensation on the membrane of my right wing, accompanied by an incredible tugging weight. I feel the skin tear, ripping and severing the delicate blood vessels. With a shriek of pain and fury, I whirl around and strike. The claws of my left hand sink deep into the dog's neck.

No.

The dog lets out a whine and steps back, shaking its head. It stares at me, accusing, before bringing up its paw as it tries to scratch at the nearly invisible marks I've just put into its flesh. It takes a staggering step. Its breath quickens, and its tongue dangles from its bloody mouth.

I take a step backward and stare at my hand. It's shaking. My whole body trembles. What have I done? I close my eyes and feel myself sway dangerously.

The sound of the dog's body thumping onto the ground is more than I can take. I turn away so I don't have to see what happens next.

I run, back under the cover of the trees, back to my spot in the woods next to the creek. My gloves lie there beneath the tree where I tossed them days ago, as if admonishing me. If I'd just worn them, this wouldn't have happened. I wouldn't have killed the dog. I wouldn't have given myself one more reminder of the monster that I am.

I shouldn't exist. This is just further proof. There's no place in this world for someone like me.

Standing there, shaking, I look down at my right arm. Blood runs down my fingers and drips from the tips of my claws. Dark flesh hangs open, dangling in glistening ribbons of shredded skin and muscles. And I can't blame the dog for it. It was just protecting its territory from a monster that had no right to be there. That has no right to be anywhere.

Well, that monster's not going to exist for much longer.

My mind is a red haze. I grab my left wing. Pull it forward. Sever the bones and muscles with my teeth. Tear through the rest of the flesh. Let it fall, splashing into the stream. It's not worth doing the same to the right one; it's bleeding and dripping, hanging limp like a set of shredded curtains, a huge chunk torn out of the membrane.

My hands rake over my head, my claws tearing at the skin, ripping open the flesh. I try to pull on my teeth, as if to yank them out of my horrible mouth, but all I get are eight sliced fingers. Before I can think about what I'm doing, I bite down hard. The fingertips, along with the hateful claws, fall to the ground, sounding like pebbles as they hit the pine needle-strewn earth. I finish with the thumbs, chewing them to a pulp before I spit them out. My hands feel like they're on fire. My skin is stinging. My right arm is cold.

I drop sideways onto the ground, not even bothering to break my fall. Biting at a loose strip of flesh on my right arm, I pull hard, screaming through my teeth until the blood gushes out and I can see the bones.

I hope it's enough. I hope, with everything that's left in me to hope, that I've done enough, and that this is the day I'll finally be free. That this is the day when the world will go back to the way it should be, where the only monsters are the ones who would condemn little boys to an eternity of misery over a bag of candy and a withheld kiss.

I awake in the depths of the night, shivering, vibrating with pain and terror as hot spikes of agony shoot down my arms and out through my fingers. I press my face into the dirt as I scream, as I claw at the pine needles with brand-new fingertips, as the skin of my right wing stretches and pulls as it knits itself back together, as a brand-new wing erupts out of the remains of the one on my left shoulder, the blistering pain like a volcano bursting through a mountain-top after centuries of dormancy. When it's over, my breath comes in audible gasps for a long time, almost sobs but not quite able to get there.

The pain burns itself out, and I fall asleep, exhausted. When I open my eyes the next day, my wings are spread over me like a blanket. One hand is just inches away from my face, almost too close to focus on, but even so, I can see the too-many-jointed fingers and the sharp little claws digging into the dirt, the hand completely unmarked, as if nothing happened.

I close my eyes again for a moment. I'm not quite ready to face the implications of this.

Finally, though, I decide I can't just lie here forever, so I push myself up and stand, brushing the forest debris from my stomach and genitals. My hands shake as I pick up my dirty gloves and slide them on. Then I walk to the edge of the woods, through the field, and across the road. By some stroke of luck, nobody sees me. At least, I'm assuming that's the case, because I don't hear any screaming or see any cars go careening off the road in an attempt to avoid my hideous form. I walk calmly back to the clearing near Tegan's house, where I crouch in my in-need-of-renovation nest and wait.

• 17 •

Full–Service Glove Detailing, While You Wait

"You've got a lot of nerve."

My head snaps up from where it rests on my knees. Tegan stands in front of me, her arms crossed, her lips twisted into a sour expression. "Me?"

"Yes, you. You think you get to come back here and pretend everything's normal?"

"I'm sorry."

She blinks. I guess she wasn't expecting that.

"Yeah, well . . . you should be." She drops her arms and sighs. "I guess you're the one the whole neighbourhood's been talking about. Creeping around in the fields, scaring the livestock, stealing chickens. Some people saw you, you know."

I shrug.

"I suppose you're hungry."

My body seems to want to collapse in on itself with shame. I pull my gloved hands against my chest and curl up as tightly as I can, resting my forehead on my knees. My wings rustle with the urge to cocoon me.

"Sam?"

I can barely breathe like this, but I don't want to move. If I look at her . . . Another wave of shame crashes over my body, and I let out a soft moan.

"Sam, are you all right? What happened?" There's a rustle of footsteps, and something warm presses up against my side. I raise my head in alarm, only to find her face just inches from my own. "What is it?"

I don't think I can say it. Swallowing hard, I flick my tongue against the back of my teeth. "The dog."

"Oh." She turns her head, but she doesn't move away. I look down at where her shoulder is pressed against mine. She's so nice and warm. I have a sudden desperate longing to put my arms around her—and maybe my wings, too—and hold on to her forever. But that might give her a heart attack, so I push the thought from my mind. "That was you?" she asks.

"Yeah."

She shakes her head. "Stan Garter was over here at five o'clock this morning, pounding on the door, accusing us of killing his stupid dog. When Dad told him we didn't have anything to do with it, he went down to the Brownings' place and accused them. He probably woke up the whole neighbourhood."

"I didn't mean to."

"What did you do, anyway? Stan said the dog wasn't injured, so it had to have been poisoned."

I pull my head down, wishing I had a shell I could disappear into like a turtle.

"Sam, what is it?"

"My claws."

"How does a dog die from being scratched?"

"They're . . . poison."

"Poison?" Her breath catches in a gasp. "And *that's* why you wear the gloves, isn't it? Omigod, Sam. Poison? You're just full of surprises, aren't you?"

"I killed a *dog*," I remind her, because she seems to have forgotten.

"Somebody would have, sooner or later. That thing was a menace. Do you know how many calls we—I mean, Dad and the neighbours—have put in to animal control about that dog? It's always getting out. It chased the Browning kids last month when they got off the bus, and it didn't back off until one of them hit it with his backpack. And it came over here and killed two of my chickens last year. It was dangerous." She looks me straight in the eye. "I'm not sorry it's gone."

"I didn't mean to," I say again. My voice is small. Tegan sighs and looks down at my hands, which are still bunched against my stomach.

"Let me see."

"What?"

"Your gloves. I want to see them."

My hands are still shaking as I pull them out from between my stomach and thighs. Tegan adjusts her position on the ground and takes both of my hands in hers. I blink in surprise, unable to believe this is happening. She frowns in concentration as she looks at the gloves, turning my hands over in hers so she can see both sides.

"What happened here?" she asks, gesturing with her chin to the slash across the back of my left glove. I click my teeth at her in answer. She raises her eyebrow. "Why would you do that?"

"I didn't do it on purpose."

"I hope not. That would just be stupid." She runs a finger over the stitching. "They're really well made. Where'd you get them?"

"They were a gift."

She lets go, and I pull my hands back into my lap. "Well, you should take better care of them." Her mouth twists as she seems to contemplate something. "I could probably fix that tear. Want me to try?"

I shake my head. "Poison."

She lets out a snort as she gets to her feet. "I can handle poison."

"No, you can't. If it gets into your bloodstream—"

"Sam, relax. I know what I'm doing. Hold tight. I'll be right back." And before I can stop her, she's gone, disappeared into the trees. My teeth click in agitation, and I lift my left hand to have another look. It *would* be nice to have it fixed, but I don't want to risk Tegan hurting herself. The poison my claws secrete has done more than enough damage already.

When she returns, she's wearing a pair of pink rubber gloves that come up to her elbows. She's carrying a tiny vial of something, along with a larger bottle, a stained rag, and what looks like an old toothbrush. At least, I hope it's an old one. I certainly wouldn't want to put its grey bristles anywhere near my mouth.

"I noticed that they're kind of . . . um . . . smelly. I thought

I'd give them a good scrub while I'm at it." She holds up the larger bottle; the label says it's some sort of leather cleaner. "Do you mind?"

I shake my head, but I hesitate. How's she going to do this? I don't want her sticking her fingers inside, even if they are covered in pink rubber.

"Hand them over."

"Be careful."

"Yes, Sam. I'll be careful. Come on." She holds one hand out expectantly.

With a deep sigh that whistles through my nostrils, I carefully pull the gloves from my hands and lay them on the ground between us. I'm certainly not about to try to hand them to her.

"Go find me a rock."

"What? Why?" My tone sounds more suspicious than I intend.

"I'm not going to hit you with it. I just need something to hold the glove open while I glue the tear."

So that's what the little vial is. I unfold myself from the nest and venture into the trees, searching the underbrush with my toes until I find something that's vaguely rock-like. "Will a pinecone work?"

"If it's big enough."

As best I can, I grasp it with my toes and half drag, half kick it back to the clearing. Tegan gives me a funny look, but doesn't say anything as she reaches for it and slides it into the main part of the glove, propping it open. Then she sets to work, uncapping the little vial and applying the transparent glue to both edges of the sliced leather.

"Where's your father?" I ask.

"At work. He won't be home until after midnight. He had to cover for someone."

I dig my toes into the loam as I look down at her, watching her pinch the two sides of the slash together. Her movements are a bit clumsy in the rubber gloves, but it's still better than I could do.

"How did you know I would be here?" I ask. She glances up with a quick smile.

"I didn't. I've been checking every day to see if you'd come back."

"*Why?*"

"Omigod, Sam. Don't sound so shocked." She doesn't look at me as she says this. Her gaze is trained on the leather in front of her. I can smell the glue now, its sharp chemical stink rising in almost-visible waves. It's a good thing we're doing this outside. "If you must know, I missed you."

"You missed me." The words sound dull in my mouth, and they make absolutely no sense.

"Of course. Didn't you miss me?"

I don't answer. She looks up with a sly grin.

"I know you did," she says. "Why else would you have come back? Unless you're just using me for food."

"No."

"See? I told you." The slash repaired, she sets the glove aside. "That stuff dries pretty quick. In the meantime . . ." She reaches for the other glove and uncaps the bottle of leather cleaner. A little dab goes onto the toothbrush, and then she's gently scrubbing the stains from the outside of my glove. I watch, feeling awkward. This really isn't her responsibility. I should've taken better care of my gloves. It's not like I have any other possessions to worry about.

It looks like this is going to take a while, so I sit back down in the nest, adjusting until my tail isn't in an awkward position. Tegan rubs at a spot between the thumb and forefinger with the cloth, her brow creasing in concentration. As she takes a deep breath and opens her mouth, I brace myself for whatever's about to come next.

"Sam, when you asked me the other day . . . Well, you asked me if I pitied you. I know I said I did, but . . . that wasn't what you meant, was it? I mean . . ." She sighs and pauses in her rubbing to look up at me. "*Why* did you ask me if I pitied you?"

"What?" I say, blinking in confusion. I'm not quite sure what she's getting at.

"It's just . . . It struck me as a strange question. I mean, I don't pity a snake for being all slithery, or a chicken for having a brain the size of a pea, or a bat for being a creepy little bugger. That's just the way they are. It's not something to be pitied. It's just . . . the way it is."

I don't say anything. She goes back to her scrubbing. For some reason, that seems to be the end of it. It's probably the first time she's ended a conversation in midstream, and it's unsettling. I watch as she sets the rag and toothbrush down and struggles to turn the glove inside out. When she realizes there's a hard metal cap in the tip of each finger, she turns an incredulous look on me. I shrug.

"The claws are sharp."

"Yeah, I'm sure they are." She pushes the pinky-finger cap

toward the palm, somehow managing to invert the finger, and peers at the foam padding within. I crane my neck, trying to get a better look. I've never actually seen the inside of my gloves before. The foam looks dense and a little shredded, but it's not as bad as I might have thought, considering I've had this pair for more than three years. She goes to work on the other fingers, and soon has all of them flipped inside out. She tugs the rest of the glove after them, then reaches for the toothbrush. I can see her nose wrinkle a bit as the nasty smell hits her. I'm catching whiffs of it from a few feet away.

How embarrassing.

"So, what have you been doing for the past week, other than scaring the living crap out of all the animals in the neighbourhood?"

"Nothing."

She finishes scrubbing down the fingers of the glove with the toothbrush, then reaches for the rag. "Really? Nothing?"

"I took a bath."

She laughs. I draw my legs closer against my body. "Well, that accounts for one afternoon. But what about the rest of the time?"

"I told you. Nothing."

As she blows out a breath, it catches a strand of her hair, sending it flying out of her face. I watch it settle back down, softly tickling her nose. She brushes it away with the back of her hand. "I don't know how you can do nothing for a week. I would be bored out of my mind."

"I *am* bored out of my mind."

"You are?" The rag stills as she looks at me. I draw back

under her gaze and nod. "What do you usually do to keep yourself occupied?"

"Usually?"

"Come off it, Sam. You're not a nature boy. I don't know where you came from, but it wasn't the woods."

"How do you know?" My voice is grumpy, on the verge of a whiny growl. Tegan holds up the inside-out glove in her hand, as if it's the obvious answer to my question.

"Maybe I just haven't met enough woodland creatures, but you're the first one I've come across who wears gloves. And these things are professionally stitched. With metal caps. And foam. I think you're more civilized than you're letting on." She gives me a sly grin before turning back to the glove, giving it one last swipe with the rag and setting it aside. The mended glove gets a good, long look before she gingerly picks it up and pokes at the leather around the glued slice. "Looks good. Told you that stuff dried fast." She shakes the pinecone onto the ground and starts to clean the outside surface of the glove. "So. Pastimes? Hobbies? Addictions?"

"Addictions?"

"Yeah. Like . . . porn. You don't have a bunch of dirty magazines tucked away in the knot of a tree or something, do you?"

When I snort, the air twists through my nostrils in a squeak. She giggles.

"Okay, no porn. But you can't tell me you've done nothing but crouch and pretend to be all creepy for seventeen years."

"I'm not pretending."

"Yes, you are. And you're not very good at it." She's gotten faster with the toothbrush. Already, she's finished with the outside. Her pink-gloved fingers struggle to invert the mended glove. "You're also not very good at answering questions. What do you do all day?" Her words are slow and deliberate, as though she's talking to a really dumb animal. I guess I am sort of giving her that impression at the moment.

"I like to read."

"You can *read?*" She nearly drops the glove in her astonished excitement. "Who taught you to read?"

I concentrate on the ground in front of my feet. My toes curl, causing my claws to leave little lines through the dirt. Before I can stop it, another memory hits me hard. In my bare feet, I leaned against Mom's side on the couch, a picture book balanced across our laps. My eyes followed the words as she read them to me in a soft voice. I was just starting to be able to pick out the combinations of letters and assign meaning to them, though I already knew the story and could recite most of the book from memory. After she turned the last page, we both said, "The end." It was sort of a tradition, and we did it with every book, whether it made sense or not. Then she shooed me into bed, where I lay thinking about all the books I was going to read one day— big ones like Mom read quietly to herself—when I grew up.

"Earth to Sam."

I blink and find Tegan staring at me, eyebrows raised. "What?"

"I asked if you wanted something to read."

I glance at her empty hands. My gloves lie side by side on the ground, still inside out. The dirty toothbrush and rag lie next to the cleaner and glue. "Are you finished?"

"Do you want something to read?"

I shrug and my wings quiver, pretty much giving away how much I really *would* like that.

"Come on, then." She gets to her feet, grabbing the cleaning supplies as she goes.

"Where?"

"I've got some books, but they're in the house." She pauses and looks down at where I'm still crouching in the destroyed nest. "You're coming with me."

My heart picks up its rhythm. "Why?"

"Because I don't want to come back out here and find you've taken off again. You're awfully flighty for someone who doesn't fly."

"I *can't* fly."

"Whatever you say." She jerks her head toward the house. "Come on."

I sigh as I unfold myself from the ground and step toward her. "You need to throw those gloves away. And the cloth. And the toothbrush."

"Well, I wasn't going to use them for my morning routine." She rolls her eyes, but when my teeth click in consternation, she sighs. "Fine. I'll throw them out. Happy?"

I don't answer, but follow her silently through the trees toward the house. She pauses by the back door to drop everything, including the bottle of cleaner and the glue, into the wheeled garbage bin that leans against the side of the house. As she peels off the pink gloves, they turn inside out. I watch them disappear into the bin, and only then do I let the air whistle from my nostrils in a sigh of relief. Quick as a bunny, she hops up the couple of steps to the back door and grasps the handle.

"Coming?" She holds open the door. Through it, I can see a dimly lit kitchen. There are no lights on—it's the middle of the day, after all—but the house is sort of dark, couched as it is in the trees. I fold my thumbs into my fists, then hold my hands tightly against my chest as I step up into the house.

Tegan walks through the room casually, as if she hasn't just invited a monster into her home. On the far side of the space, she flicks a switch, and a yellowed light fixture buzzes to life above our heads.

"I feel like I should offer you a snack or something," she says, eyeing the fridge. "But I doubt there's anything in there you'd want." She pauses. "We've got eggs, though. Would you like an egg?"

My stomach tries to answer for me, but I talk over it. "No, thanks."

"Okay. Come on." She turns toward the doorway that leads to a darkened hallway.

"Where?"

"My room, silly. That's where all my books are."

I don't move. My wings pull tight against my back as I try to make myself as small as possible. Tegan shakes her head with a smile and reaches for my hand. I snap my teeth at her, and she jumps back, startled.

"Sorry. I forgot." Beckoning with her hand, she turns and slips into the hallway. I feel ridiculously out of place standing in the kitchen, and I know it isn't going to be any better in any other room in this house, but I suspect I'll feel even sillier if I continue to stand here by myself. So I follow her as she ascends the stairs and emerges into an even darker hallway at the top. She turns left and pushes open a door. I follow her inside.

I've never been inside a girl's bedroom. Actually, I've never been inside any normal teenager's bedroom. I take everything in with wide eyes. There's a cozy-looking bed that's shoved under the sloping ceiling. I can't tell if it's supposed to be made or not; if it is, she didn't do a very good job. On the other side of the room, a white desk is strewn with papers, open textbooks, and a number of cords for various electronic devices. My clawed toes click on the wooden floor until I step onto a fuzzy purple rug that feels almost as soft as feathers under my feet. A large window is flanked by yellow curtains that have been thrown wide, letting in a shaft of sunlight that seems to have found a clear path through the trees.

"The books are back here," she says, nudging me out of the way so she can close the door and get at the squat bookcase behind it. As the door swings shut, the movement seems to multiply, and suddenly there are more than the two of us in the room. I let out a strangled shriek and jump back, teeth clicking in panic. Tegan whirls around, her eyes wide.

"Sam? What . . . ?"

My heart should be calming down, now that I know it's just a mirror. But it can't. It can't . . . because of what I see staring back at me. This is what everyone else sees. This is what *she* sees. I take a step forward, my breath hitching in disbelief.

Dr. Grant never allowed me to be around any mirrors, so the only glimpses I've gotten of myself over the years have been distorted and dark, reflections in doorknobs or flat surfaces that are too dull to really show me my own horrible form. And it *is* horrible. I take a step closer to the mirror, unable to tear my gaze away from the abomination I see before me.

The face is the worst part. *My* face. Though the top part of my head is shaped pretty much like a human's, the lower half definitely isn't. The lipless maw stretches long, tapering more than a human mouth should. The teeth are black, crowded, and sharp, and so large that even if my lips hadn't curled up and disappeared during the transformation, they wouldn't have been able to cover the two rows of deadly, knife-like points. As I watch, I can see the skin of my nostrils quiver as I breathe. Featureless black eyes blink back at me, two dark pools that seem to have their own magnetic pull.

"Sam?"

She's still in here with me. How can she be? How can she have let me—this *thing*—into her bedroom? Isn't she afraid of having nightmares? Isn't she afraid of . . . me?

I slowly lift my wings. The sun lights them from behind, illuminating the network of blood vessels within the translucent membranes. As the tip of one wing brushes against the papers on the desk, it knocks a couple of them to the floor. I quickly furl my wings again and turn away from the mirror.

"Sorry."

"It's not a big deal." She grabs the papers and tosses them back on the desk before returning to the bookcase and crouching down in front of it. I know my behaviour in front of the mirror wasn't normal, but, for some reason, she's not bringing it up. That can't be a good sign.

"Maybe I should go."

"Sam, sit your ass down and be quiet. You're not going anywhere." She looks up at me, and I blink helplessly.

"Sit?"

"Yes, sit. Or squat. Whatever." She waves her hand at the bed. "Don't just stand there."

I cast around desperately, my gaze falling on the desk chair (which has a back that'll interfere with my tail), the bed (I'm not about to sit my naked butt on her bed), and the fluffy rug. I fall into a crouch, curling my toes into the purple pile.

"What kind of stuff do you usually read?" She's turned away as she studies the spines on the shelf, so she can't see me shrug. I'm going to have to answer.

"Anything."

"Not very discerning, eh?"

"I read what I can get."

She doesn't say anything to that, but pulls a couple of hardcovers from the shelf and stands back up. "I think you'll like these ones." The way she says it makes me think I probably won't.

"What are they about?"

She holds up one with a dark cover. A winged man holding a sword stands protectively beside a young woman in a frilly dress. "This one's about a fallen angel who comes to Earth to seek revenge on those who caused him to be cast out of Heaven."

"Who's the girl?"

"She's the one who falls in love with the angel."

I let out a wheezing snort. "What about the other book?"

"Oh . . ." She grins slyly. "I'm not going to spoil that one for you." She holds the books out toward me, but I shake my head and raise my fisted hands.

"Poison."

"Oh. Right." She shakes her head and tosses the books onto her bed. Sitting down next to them on the rumpled red bedspread, she sighs. "I forgot."

"How could you forget?"

"I don't know. I just did." She shrugs, but I can tell there's something she isn't saying. "I'll walk you back later and bring the books. You can read them when you put your gloves back on."

"You'll walk me back *later?*"

She leans forward. "What? You don't like being in my room?"

If I could blush, I think I would. Instead, I stare down at the rug and clear my throat. "It's . . . nice."

"Nicer than yours?"

I keep my gaze on the rug. "I don't have a room."

"You're a terrible liar, Sam. It's going to get you into trouble one of these days."

I think of Aunt Adelijda and her loaded questions. It's not like the truth has done me any favours, either.

"You want to know what I think?"

"Not really."

"Sure you do, Sam. Okay. I think you're not being entirely honest about where you came from. And I think . . ." She pauses dramatically. I hold my breath. "I think you probably *are* the only one of your kind."

"Why do you say that?" My heart is pounding so loudly

I'm sure she must be able to hear it. I adjust my wings, hoping the rustle will cover up some of the racket.

"Well, first of all, you can speak English, even though you can't make all the sounds. So I think that maybe it's not your native language."

I give a non-committal humph and dig my toes in further. I feel my claws come up against the rug's stiff backing.

"Second, you can read. Somebody must've taught you.

"Third," she goes on, not waiting for me to react, "you wear those cool gloves, which are professionally made. You said they were a gift, and I'm going to assume there isn't this hidden glove factory out in the middle of the forest staffed by squirrels, so that means whoever gave them to you was probably . . . um . . . someone like me."

"Human."

"Yes. Human. And fourth, judging by the way you just freaked out when you saw your own reflection, I'm guessing you haven't actually seen anyone else like you."

I can't look at her. She's so precariously close to discovering the truth—the *whole* truth—and I'm not sure if I'm ready for that.

"You said your father was alive, but . . ."

"I don't know if he is."

"Oh, Sam." She slides off the bed to sit in front of me on the rug. Her voice is so full of sympathy that I feel like crying. But of course I can't. I click my teeth and turn away from her gaze. "That's the other thing," she says, her voice gentle. "When you asked me if I pitied you, I couldn't understand why. But now I think I do. It's because you don't know anyone else like you. You weren't raised by your own kind, were you? You were raised by humans. But, Sam," she says, getting up onto her knees and leaning forward, "you can't compare yourself to us. We're different. We just are. There's nothing wrong with that."

"There's *everything* wrong with that," I say, the growl bursting out of me before I can stop it. She sits back on her heels.

"Sam, are you ashamed of what you are?"

Of course I am. I turn my head back to look at her, and when I see her perfectly human features, her blunt white teeth working on her lower lip as she waits for my answer, the shame sweeps over me in a renewed wave. "I don't want to be like this."

"But you are."

I am. I wear my childhood mistake where everyone can see it and judge it. Judge *me*. I am a rat snacker, a chicken eater, a dog killer. I don't want to be. But I have no choice. I have no choice because I made the wrong one when I was seven years old. And I will never have a choice about what I become because I don't have a choice about what I am.

Tegan is right. We're different. Too different. Maybe not too different to be friends. But definitely too different to break the curse.

"I think I should go now," I say.

"Sam . . ." Her voice trails off as she watches me stand. I disentangle my toe claws from the rug and step to the door, waiting for her to open it for me.

"Please," I say.

"Okay." Slowly, she stands up and reaches for the books on her bed. Then she opens the door, and we head back downstairs to the kitchen. As I wait by the back door, she hastily pulls open the fridge and grabs a small carton of eggs. I shake my head, but she just mirrors the movement back at me. "You need to eat, Sam. I don't want you getting desperate and deciding you want to eat Letitia and Fergus."

"Who?"

"The goats." She holds the back door open for me, and I stumble out into the waning afternoon.

"I wouldn't."

She says little else as we walk back to my clearing. My gloves are where we left them. I pick them up and start to wiggle the fingers back the right side out.

"Do you need help?" she asks.

"I can manage."

"Okay." She pauses, unsure, then bends down and sets the books on the ground, the egg carton on top. "Enjoy your snack. And the books."

"Thank you."

She twists her fingers together in front of her. "Sam, I didn't mean to upset you."

"You didn't." It's true. All she did was point out the truth. And it wasn't news to me.

"Are you sure?"

"Yes." I wish I could smile at her. But with my mouth fixed in this permanent macabre grin—I shudder a little as I remember what I saw in the mirror—that's not an option. "Goodnight, Tegan."

"Night, Sam."

I don't see her go. I struggle with the gloves for a few more minutes before finally getting them inverted and back on my hands. As I bring them up to my face, I inhale deeply. All I can smell is the cleaner she used on them, but now the scent is connected with her in my mind. I take another deep breath and close my eyes with a sigh. Then I get to work tidying my nest.

I want to at least have a comfortable place to read.

• 18 •

A Voracious Reader

When I wake up the next morning, my wings feel frozen. The dead leaves around me are rimed with frost; the ones closest to my body have turned into a brown mush that smells of decay. I stand up, hoping my brittle-feeling limbs don't snap like frozen twigs, and walk around the clearing a few times, vigorously flapping my wings to try to get the blood flowing. I rise up on my toes for a moment, feeling strangely buoyant. When I fold the wings against my back, my heels sink to the ground.

The eggs are chilly in their little cardboard carton. There are five nestled into their divots, leaving one empty spot. I eat three of them, tossing them back like the jelly beans I used to love as a kid, and close the carton back up before setting it aside. The book with the ridiculously handsome angel on the cover sits on top. I slide it carefully to the side and pick up the other one. I have no idea what it's about, and since the dust jacket is missing, I have no way of finding out until I read it. The expression Tegan wore yesterday when she offered me the book makes me a little wary, but . . . let's face it. I have nothing else to do.

Since returning, since being around her, I feel . . . more like myself. I don't know what happened out there by that creek, but I don't even like to think about it now. Going for days without speaking; gorging myself on live chickens; killing the dog; mutilating my own body in that unspeakable, self-loathing rage . . . Looking back, it was like I'd temporarily lost . . . something. The thought that I might lose it again terrifies me. When I settle myself down in the lukewarm nest, gripping the book tightly in my gloved hands as if it's my last connection to the human world, I promise myself I'm going to make the most of these last days before the inevitable end. While there's still a chance, no matter how small, that the curse can be broken, I'm going to hold on to my dream of being human again. When November first comes . . . well, then, I guess I'll have to let it go. But I can make the choice to be civilized now. I can be Tegan's friend for a few more days. Even though I know, deep down, nothing will come of it and I'm just deluding myself, the thought of enjoying all these normal things—books, conversation, friendship—brings me a sort of comfort that warms me from the tips of my webbed toes to the top of my smooth, blackened scalp.

I'm a pretty fast reader, having taught myself a form of speed reading when I was eleven (what else did I have to occupy my time?), so I make it through the first half of the book almost faster than my awkwardly gloved fingers can turn the pages. By the time I'm three quarters of the way through, my hands are gripping the sides of the book in what would be a white-knuckled grip if I had human skin. A few pages from the end, I realize I'm breathing heavily, noisily. When I turn the last page and close the cover, I just stare at it. Any sense of comfort I might have felt before is gone, replaced with an awful, gnawing hopelessness.

Why would she give me this book? Was it supposed to be a joke? Why is she rubbing my non-existent nose in . . . this?

With a shriek, I tear the book in two, severing it down the length of its spine. My gloved fingers fumble as they grab for the pages. In frustration, I grab the paper with my teeth, ripping it with a satisfying sound. Half-torn pages flutter to the ground like giant confetti, and I throw the mostly intact half of the book as far as I can into the trees. I toss back my head and let loose a sharp shriek that sounds like frustration and anger and loss all rolled into one.

When I calm down, I realize I've just attacked a book. A freaking *book*. What is wrong with me? I mean, besides the obvious. Looking at the ground, my eyes take in the torn white pages, scattered like leaves around my feet. I reach for the nearest one. The page number squats in the lower right corner. Maybe . . .

A minute later, I'm on my hands and knees, trying to put together the most boring puzzle ever. I've got a few of the pages back in the right order, but even more of them remain scattered and mysterious, unplaceable without any sort of numbers or obvious markings. I barely notice the rustle of footsteps.

"Sam! Are you all right? I heard you—" Tegan breaks off. I look up into her astonished face. "Is that my book?"

Half of it, anyway. "I'm sorry." The apology sounds so feeble, so inadequate. "I'll fix it."

She steps farther into the clearing, careful not to tread on any of the page bits. "I think it's beyond fixing." With a shake of her head, she folds her arms across her chest. "Got some impulse-control issues, do you?"

"No." I click my teeth in frustration. "Yes."

"Which is it?"

I sigh and turn back to the impossible puzzle. "I didn't like the ending."

"Omigod, Sam." She lets out a breath and drops into a crouch in front of me before reaching for one of the pieces near her foot. "Remind me to warn the library about you. They're not going to want to give you a library card if this is what happens when you don't like an ending."

"I'm sorry."

"Yeah. I know." She stacks a few pieces together in a little pile, her fingers hesitant, as if she's thinking about something else while she's doing this. "What was so bad about it? I thought you'd like it."

A bark of bitter laughter escapes me. "You thought I'd like a story about a girl who falls in love with a supernatural creature?"

"Um . . . yeah." She says this like it should be obvious to me. "What's wrong with—"

"You thought it would give me hope or something?"

She presses her lips together and looks down at the pile, but she doesn't touch it.

"Dornan was a *handsome* demon," I say. "He looked human. Layla was physically attracted to him. That's just . . ."

"What?" Her voice is barely a whisper.

I look down at the pathetic pile of paper in front of me. She's right. It's beyond fixing. "Unrealistic. It's unrealistic."

"It's just a story, Sam."

I stare at her in wide-eyed disbelief. Maybe it is just a story. But my life isn't. It's real, and it sucks.

It *hurts*.

"It's kind of a silly book, anyway," she says at last. "I . . . don't have much else. I can get you something from the library. Tell me what you like, and I'll get it."

"Never mind. I'll probably just eat those books, too."

"You *ate* some of it?"

"No. Well, maybe a tiny bit." I carefully run my tongue over the back of my teeth, near the gumline, checking for any bits of paper that might've gotten stuck.

"Omigod." She stands up, and I'm afraid she's upset. But when I look up at her face, I see that it looks more like she's trying not to laugh.

"What?"

"I've heard of people devouring books. But I don't think this is what they meant."

· 19 ·

Movie Night

The smell of popcorn hits me before I see her trudging through the trees. She's got a flashlight in one hand and a swollen bag of microwave popcorn in the other, and when she steps into the clearing, I can make out the straps of the backpack on her shoulders. I stand up, abandoning my nest, and walk forward to meet her.

"You up for movie night?" she asks, handing me the flashlight while she takes off the backpack and very carefully sets it on the ground.

"Right now?"

"No. We're going to have movie night in the middle of the day." I don't have to see her roll her eyes to know she's doing it. "Yes, right now. I brought snacks and everything."

"I can't eat—" I break off as I see her pull a small plastic container with three eggs out of the backpack, along with a tablet and a gaudy patterned blanket.

"See? I've thought of everything."

"What about your father?"

"He's fast asleep. Has been for hours. These long shifts are killing him." She shakes out the blanket and spreads it over the ground. "I don't think he'd wake up for the apocalypse at this point."

She sits down on the blanket and opens the egg container and popcorn bag before setting them within easy reach in front of her. As she pulls the tablet into her lap and turns it on, she glances up at me.

"Sit down."

"I . . ."

"Omigod, Sam. Just sit, will you? Or don't. But turn off the flashlight. It's causing glare on the screen." She turns back to the tablet and brings up a familiar-looking app. It's one I've used many times myself, whiling away the lonely hours in my room, trying to keep myself entertained with stories about a world I would never get to experience for myself. Finally, I find the button on the flashlight and snap it off. Then I step onto the blanket.

"Any requests?" She angles the menu screen toward me as I gingerly sit down next to her. My wings are too big to stay comfortably folded in this position, so I spread them out a little, careful to keep them from bumping the backs of her shoulders.

"No romance," I say.

"That's not a request. That's like . . . an anti-request."

"No chick flicks."

"Anything else?"

I think for a moment. "No tearjerkers."

She sighs. "Well, that just about eliminates all of my favourites." She swipes her finger absently over the screen, scanning the titles. "What's your favourite movie?"

"I don't have one."

She lets out a little cough of annoyance. "Remember what I said about lying, Sam? Don't give me some garbage about how you've never seen a movie. I know you have. The fact that you just referred to chick flicks and tearjerkers gave you away."

Crap.

"I don't have one favourite," I say. "I like lots of movies."

"Such as . . ."

I mention a few, but she just shakes her head.

"I haven't heard of any of those." She sighs. "Great. I'm about to get roped into watching some obscure drama that you'll have to explain to me afterward, aren't I?"

"We could always watch *The Wizard of Oz*," I say.

"Really?" Her voice is almost dripping with disbelief.

"There's no romance, and it's not that sad. Plus, I have a real affinity with some of the characters."

"Who? The scarecrow? The lion?"

"No. The flying monkeys."

She goes still and, for a moment, doesn't say anything. Then she turns to me, as if to check if I'm being serious. I give my wings a gentle flap, and her hair flies in wisps around her face. With a grin, she turns back to the tablet and finds the movie. As it begins to play through the opening credits, she props the tablet up in front of us on the blanket and edges closer until she's pressed right up against me. I hug my knees and lean forward, preparing to distract myself with cyclones and yellow brick roads and magic shoes that can take you wherever you want to go. With a start, I realize I wouldn't need magic shoes to do that. There's nowhere else I really want to be.

Both of us get so engrossed in the movie that we completely forget about the snacks until Dorothy wakes up back in Kansas. After Tegan turns the tablet off, I indulge in one of the eggs, tossing it high in the air and catching it between my teeth with a satisfying crunch. She copies me with her popcorn, and misses. Over and over again.

"You're not very good at this," I say.

"Yeah, well, I don't have a massive mouth. You've got the advantage in this game."

I open my mouth wide to show her just how big it is, then close my jaws with a snap. She doesn't even flinch.

"It's not the size of your mouth," I say. "Your aim just sucks."

"Oh, yeah? I'd like to see you do any better."

Is that a challenge? I glance at the open bag of popcorn, then back at her. She opens her mouth. When I don't move, she closes it again and gives me a withering look.

"Chicken?"

"I'd love one."

"No, I mean . . ." She dissolves into giggles as she takes a handful of popcorn from the bag and dumps it into my palm. "Let's see how good your aim is. Go!"

My first shot at her open mouth is embarrassingly inaccurate, but that's probably because my hands are shaking so much. The second one comes a little closer, hitting her on the cheek. The third hits her in the eye.

"Come on, Sam! I'm *starving*."

I get up onto my knees so I'm at a better angle. This time, the fluffy white kernel flies straight into her mouth. She crunches down on it with a wide grin.

"Okay, one out of four isn't bad, but it isn't great." When she opens her mouth again, I throw the whole handful at her. She laughs as she shakes the popcorn out of her hair. "A couple even made it into my mouth! Actually, that might be a more efficient way of doing things . . ." Before I know what's happening, she's launched a whole handful of popcorn at my head. I feel one of the pieces stick in my nostril, and I can sort of see it suspended there, between my eyes. When I blow it away with a huff of air, it goes flying. Tegan loses it. She flops onto her back, laughing so hard she can barely breathe.

"Omigod. Ouch . . . my stomach." She presses her hands against her sides and tries to take a deep, steady breath. But when she looks over at me again, she bursts into another peal of laughter.

I'm trying to remember this, recording it all onto the celluloid of my mind so I can play it back later: The way I feel as I watch her. Her laugh, the sound like jingling bells. The smell of popcorn. The sensation of sitting next to her in silence as we lost ourselves in a magical story, feeling her body so close to mine. It's a movie I know I'm going to want to watch over and over again in the years to come. I purposely leave out the hope I can feel bubbling in my guts. That's something I won't want to be reminded of.

As Tegan slowly calms down, her giggles peter out and she lies there, staring up at the sky. Her hair is loose, spread out around her head. I have an urge to touch it, to run my fingers through it. As if she's somehow picking up on my thoughts, she reaches up and pulls her hair into a ponytail, then releases it, only to start playing with one silky strand, wrapping it around and around her finger.

"I guess I should go back inside," she says at last. Her head turns toward me. "I need to get a few hours of sleep."

I nod. She sits up and grabs the tablet and the half-empty popcorn bag, then reaches for the backpack.

"I'm going to leave the blanket. It's getting cold out here." She pauses in the middle of unzipping the backpack. "What are you going to do when winter comes?"

I shrug. I haven't really thought that far ahead.

"Your kind don't . . . um . . . fly south for the winter, do you?"

"Cancun."

"Really?"

"No."

She shakes her head with a smile and turns back to the backpack. After shoving the tablet into a padded pocket, she pulls something else out of the main compartment. "Here."

I gape. In her hands is a brown teddy bear. I vaguely remember seeing it sitting on top of her bookshelf. "What's that for?"

"For you." She shrugs. "I know it's silly, but . . . I just thought that maybe it wouldn't seem so lonely out here if you had something to hold on to."

I click my teeth. "I'm seventeen." My gaze flickers over the bear in her outstretched hand. "Besides, do you really want to give me that? Did you forget what I did to your book?"

"No, I haven't forgotten. And I'm well aware that I might

return to find Fredo's fluffy guts all over the forest floor. But he's yours now. You can tear his head off for stress release, if that's what you want to do."

When I still don't make a move to take the bear, she places it on the blanket next to the egg container. It sits there in the darkness, staring with blank, beady eyes.

"I might not be able to come and see you for a few days." She stands up and swings the backpack onto one shoulder. The popcorn bag crumples in her hands. "School is getting intense now, and Dad's getting a little suspicious. He already thinks I'm too much of a homebody. He wants me to spend more time with my friends. Like . . . school friends."

I nod slowly.

"It's just that, if I don't at least make a good show of it, he's going to know something's up. So I'm going to be doing some stuff with my friend Krissy this weekend."

"Okay."

"I'll be back as soon as I can. If you get hungry . . ." She trails off, looking a little lost.

"I'll be fine for a few days." I gesture to the eggs. "I'll make them last."

"Okay. Well. Goodnight, then."

"Goodnight, Tegan."

As she makes her way back to her house, I survey the clearing. The white popcorn strewn all over the ground almost glows in the dim light. The moon has come out from behind a cloud, and though it's not full, it's still bright. I can make out the eggs in their little container. And the bear. The stupid bear.

Setting the eggs aside, I shake the popcorn from the

blanket and pull it over to my nest, ignoring the stuffed animal and letting it tumble onto the ground, where it lies on its side in the dirt. As I tug the blanket around my furled wings, trying to cover as much of my body as I can, I can feel the bear's plastic eyes watching me.

Dr. Grant never gave me any stuffed animals. I don't know if he thought I was too old for them, or what. But I hadn't quite outgrown them. I never told him this, but for the first six months after my arrival at the hospital, I missed my stuffed rabbit, Hercules, so much that I would wad up my blanket and hug it against my chest, pretending my old friend was with me. It was never the same, though. A knot of blanket didn't have soft ears that I could grasp in my hands, thread whiskers that tickled my cheek when I held him close, or knobby scars from Mom's mending attempts that I used to rub with my thumb while I told him my secrets.

After lying there for a while, cocooned in wings and blanket and still unable to sleep, I crawl over until I can reach out and snatch Fredo by the ear. As I curl up under the blanket once more, I hold the bear against my chest. It's the first time I've hugged anything like this in nearly eleven years. My arms ache with longing as they tighten around the lifeless teddy, and I press my face against its plush body, breathing in the scent of my only friend.

• 20 •

Meeting the Kids

I try to make the angel book last, but it's difficult to slow down when I'm so used to reading quickly. It's not a challenging read, anyway, with its simple language and even simpler plot. When I get to the halfway mark, I close it and set it aside. The book is even more ridiculous than the one I shredded.

If such a thing is possible.

I spend the rest of my first solitary morning tidying my clearing. The leaves of my nest get torn out and replaced with new ones that haven't been repeatedly frozen and then thawed by the warmth of my body. It's difficult to find enough to work with; the woods are getting bare, and the leaves that fell a few weeks earlier are in various states of decay. When I've done all I can with the nest, I go to work on the clearing itself, painstakingly picking up the popcorn and placing it in a pile near the entry point that Tegan usually uses. I'm not quite sure what to do with it. After a night out in the dew and damp, it doesn't look very appetizing; then again, it didn't look very appetizing to me in the first place. And there's yet another thing I've lost. I used to love popcorn, especially the greasy yellow stuff that I was only allowed to have when Mom and Dad took me to the movie theatre. As I drop the last pieces onto the little hill of soggy white fluff, I wonder to myself if the chickens would like it. I'd better check with Tegan first, though; I don't want to accidentally kill her birds.

She didn't say whether her father was going to be home or not, but when I slink over to the house and peer at the driveway, I figure it's a pretty safe assumption he's not there. His truck—which I can hear rattling through the trees whether he's coming or going—is nowhere to be seen. The house is closed up tight, and all the lights are turned off. I hope Tegan's having fun with her friends. I'm sure she is; they've got to be a lot more sociable than me.

I lurch around the back of the house toward the barn. The chicken coop is open, and the birds are milling about their fenced-in yard . . . but when they sense me coming, they get all hot and bothered. Feathers fly as they trip over each other in their frenzy. But I'm not interested in them today. At least, I tell myself I'm not, though my salivary glands have other ideas. I wipe the string of drool with my forearm and try to ignore the food scattering loudly across the yard.

The air in the barn is heady and moist, and I can tell right away that I'm in the presence of other living creatures. I move past the empty stalls, which might have once housed other animals. Between the dim light coming in through the open door and the grimier light shining through the taped window at the back, there's just enough to illuminate my surroundings. There are tools I don't recognize, equipment I couldn't name, and dust everywhere. It floats, suspended in the light, tickling my nostrils until I sneeze with a loud squeak. Something in the back corner of the last stall rustles.

The two goats have two very different reactions when they see me standing there, though neither is what I expect. A small one wearing a pink collar—which I assume is Letitia—stands in the corner facing me, her eyes dark against her white hair. She turns her head slightly away, as if to contemplate me better. She doesn't move. I don't actually see Fergus until he rams his head into my left knee.

Taking a staggering step to the side, I click my teeth and hiss at the black-and-white goat. He backs up, his feet whispering against the straw. As I look back and forth between them, my stomach lets out an ominous growl.

"No," I say to it, as if I'm calmly trying to talk down a wild animal. I guess, in a way, I am. "Letitia and Fergus are *not* for eating." Maybe if I keep reminding myself of their names, the desire to sink my teeth into them will dissipate.

Although, that didn't work out so well for Linda the chicken.

I hold one gloved hand out toward Letitia as I fall into a crouch. She sniffs, taking a step closer. When she's within reach, I touch my gloved fingers to the top of her head, right between her little horns. I smile inwardly as I think about that, and realize my situation could be—marginally—worse. I could have horns growing out of the top of my head, too.

"See?" I say. "I'm not going to eat you." Not today, anyway. After November first, though, all bets are off. Which reminds me . . . I need to check with Tegan the next time I see her and find out how close my doom is.

Fergus lets out a shuddering bleat and turns in a circle, agitated. Letitia's warmed up to me, though. I have a strange suspicion that Fergus might be jealous.

"You guys aren't ashamed of being goats, are you?" I say, still rubbing the top of Letitia's head. She leans into my hand and steps closer. "That's 'cause it's all you've ever known. You don't know there are other things you could be. You don't know what you're missing by not being anything else." I pause. "But you're not really missing anything, are you? You've got a nice set-up here. A cozy place to sleep. An owner who feeds you regularly. And you've got each other. You'll go on to have kids, and they'll look just like their parents—"

My voice cuts off, and my hand falls away from Letitia's head. She protests, loudly. I sit down in the straw, crushing my tail under me.

"What would you do without Fergus?" I ask Letitia. She stares blankly, her lash-rimmed eyes fixed on my hand as she steps closer. "What if you were the only goat left on Earth?" She nudges my hand, her teeth nibbling at my glove. I pull it out of her reach. "You'd be lonely, Letitia. You'd be so lonely you wouldn't be able to stand it. But you'd have to, because you can't change the way things are. You couldn't stop being a goat, and you couldn't make any other goats magically appear. You'd just have to suck it up and endure it."

I turn to Fergus. "So don't leave her. You guys need to

stick together. You don't realize it, because you're just a stupid goat, but you'd miss her if she was gone. And she'd miss you. So don't do anything stupid and get yourself killed or . . ." I trail off. I'm not sure *why* Tegan and her father have goats. Letitia doesn't look particularly milk-worthy, and Fergus is just stringy. I have a feeling that this is *not* how one would run a professional goat business, so Letitia and Fergus are probably just pets. Very smelly pets, but to each their own.

As if he can sense my thought—and is horribly insulted—Fergus decides to take another run at me. His head smashes into my shoulder, and my wings unfurl in surprise.

"I just told you not to do anything stupid," I say, rubbing my shoulder with my hand. Fergus lets out a noise that sounds like an old car trying (and failing) to turn over. I narrow my eyes at him. "Don't be a jerk."

• 21 •

Memories in the Mist

After spending hours chatting with the goats (during which Fergus headbutts me four more times; I think I must be growing on him), I wander back to my clearing, brushing the itchy straw from my limbs. I eat one of the eggs left over from movie night, but it doesn't do much about my stomach's loud hunger. The angel book sits with the folded blanket, kept company by Fredo, but if I start reading it again now, I'm so bored that I'll probably finish by the time it's dark, and then I'll have nothing to do tomorrow. I hope Tegan hasn't forgotten about getting me some new reading material from the library.

The last thing I feel like reading about right now is a handsome boy with wings.

Finally, unable to think of any better way to pass my time, I peel off my gloves and set them on Fredo's head. As I reach for the nearest large tree trunk, I'm reminded of when I did this before. It feels like years ago, but it's only been a couple of weeks. This time, though, I have nothing to prove. I don't plan on jumping, and I certainly don't plan on flying. I'm just bored . . . so I dig my claws into the bark and begin to climb.

When I reach the first branches, I'm almost twenty feet off the ground. I keep going, pulling myself higher and higher, wrapping my elongated fingers around the branches I can reach, shimmying up the trunk through the branchless stretches. As I get higher, I can feel the tree moving, a gentle sway in the still autumn air. The view of the ground is partially obscured by the tree's needles. I have no idea what kind of tree it is, and it doesn't matter. It just feels good to climb. If I fall . . . so what? My body will heal, and I'll be back to my same monstrous self by the time Tegan returns in a couple of days.

I know she's coming back—actually, I'm pretty sure the only thing that would stop her from coming back and annoying me some more is death itself—and yet I'm still anxious. I guess when you've only got one person you can depend on, you tend to get a little clingy.

What would happen if she didn't come back?

I push away the thought as I shimmy higher, my knees hugging the rough bark. I think about Dr. Grant, and how I depended on him, too . . . but in a different way. He took care of my basic needs—food, shelter, my gloves—but there was always something missing. For almost eleven years, he was the only father I knew . . . and yet he treated me more like a pet than a son.

And, so what? Should I be surprised that he never

thought of me as anything more than a medical curiosity? I'm not human anymore. Why should he have treated me like one?

Sighing, my arms shaking from exertion, I pull myself up onto a branch and lean sideways against the trunk. Beyond my dangling feet, I can see the ground far below me, visible only in small patches between the dull green of the needled branches. The tree sways gently, creaking like an old rocking chair.

From up here, I can almost see over the treetops. Tegan's house is nearly invisible from this vantage point, hidden behind overlapping branches. I rest my head against the rough bark as I stare off toward the west, watching the sky darken. There's no spectacular sunset tonight, just a slowly dimming blue-grey expanse that seems to bring a chill air with it.

I curl my legs back around the branch until my heels touch my dangling tail, then swing them forward again. For a horrible moment, the swaying of the tree combines with my own movement, and I feel like I've lost my balance. I throw my arm around the trunk and dig my claws in, but there's really no need. I'm still perched squarely on the branch, safe, even though I don't really feel like I am.

It actually would be amazing to be able to fly. To always have a way to get from place to place, no matter where it was. To not have to be afraid of falling. Still with one arm around the trunk, I spread my wings wide. Why would I have them if they weren't meant to be used?

Why do I have claws? Why do I have a humped back? Why do I have a tail? There is no reason, other than to make the curse as punishing as possible. For the first time in a while, I allow myself to think about Aunt Adelijda and what she did to me.

It wasn't fair. I know that, but I still blame myself, because there was something I could have done to prevent all of this. If I had just thanked her with a kiss, I wouldn't have undergone the transformation. My mother would still be alive. My father would still be in my life. I would probably be going to school—no, wait . . . I would have graduated in June. So I would be in university now, starting on my dream of becoming a doctor. I might even have a girlfriend.

But Aunt Adelijda took all of that away from me with one spark of her finger on the tip of my nose. And for what? Even now, it seems like an overreaction, the curse completely out of proportion to my childish faux pas.

I think about what Tegan said regarding pitying those who hurt other people. Pitying them because they've been hurt themselves. For the first time, I wonder what happened to Aunt Adelijda to make her so cruel that she would condemn me to all that she has. What pain in her past was she trying to pass on to me, as if sharing the burden would make it easier to bear? I suppose it doesn't matter. She's dead, and now the burden of all that pain rests upon my ugly, curved shoulders.

The sun is gone, and the still evening air prickles my skin with the cold. Very carefully, I start to make my way back down to the ground, feeling my way in the darkening shade of the tree's branches. When I'm about three-quarters of the way down, my arms don't have the strength to hold me anymore. I try to hold on, and my claws scrape helplessly against the bark as I fall parallel to the trunk, plummeting toward the earth. When I hit, I hear delicate ankle bones snap, and I fall back onto my wings, a harsh laugh the only sound I allow to escape.

I drag myself backward until I can reach my things. The blanket gets laid gently over my throbbing legs. Fredo gets clutched to my chest. Then I close my eyes and wait for the curse to do what it does best: keep this body healthy enough to last an eternity.

"Sammy."

The voice pulls me from sleep. I throw off the blanket and watch it float to the ground far below. My toes curl around the branch, claws digging in. I don't remember climbing up here again, but I must have. My eyes swivel, taking in the mist that swirls in eddies beneath me. It's white, almost glowing in the darkness. But it's not quite as bright as the glow coming from the tree trunk next to me, a sparkling line of light that glimmers around the edges of what looks like a door. There's no handle, so I reach out and knock. The door swings inward, and the light momentarily blinds me. I throw up my hands to shield my eyes.

"Oh, Sammy."

My hands fall from my face, and I find myself standing in a starlit field, waist-deep in silently quivering weeds. The mist curls around me, and around the figure that stands just inches away. I begin to reach out, but my arms feel like lead, and I can barely move. I look up into the figure's face, certain now that I'm locked inside a dream. But, at that moment, I don't really care.

"Mom?"

"Yes, baby. It's me." She smiles, and I want to smile in return. But I can't. Even in a dream, I can't. Even in a dream, I'm locked in this abominable body.

"I'm so sorry, Mom. I'm so sorry." I glance down at my hands, which hang lifeless at my sides. The gloves are on, eleven years too late for the woman standing in front of me. But she shakes her head, hushing me with a soft whisper. Her brown curls brush against her shoulders, and I long to give one of them a gentle tug, the way I sleepily used to do when she rocked me in her arms.

"No, baby. It's all right. It wasn't your fault. You didn't know what would happen. None of us did."

Her gaze is steady and direct, not at all flinching. This isn't right. She should be scared. Or at least worried. But, as she reaches out toward me, resting her palm against the side of my face, all I know is warmth and acceptance. I close my eyes.

"I'm so proud of you, Sammy." Her voice is gentle, but strong. I open my eyes in time to see her other hand come up to join the first. Her thumbs brush over my cheekbones, and she looks straight into my eyes. "You've been so brave for so long. This burden never should have been yours to bear. I'm sorry I couldn't protect you, baby. I'm so sorry. But you've done so well." She steps forward and kisses my forehead. She barely even has to tilt her head up; I really am hunched.

"Mom, I'm scared."

She draws back, looking so sad. "I know, baby. I know."

"What am I going to do? I can't break the curse. Not like this. And I can't . . . I don't want to be in this body forever. I'll lose myself. I don't want to become a monster. And I will. If I have to stay in this body, I know I will. There's no escape. I can't even die!"

"Sammy." Her hands move to my shoulders as she stands before me, her gaze boring into mine. "You are not immortal."

"Yes, I am. I should have died more than once already. I can't bleed to death. I heal too quickly."

She's quiet for a moment, the expression on her face thoughtful yet sad. "You're not immortal, Sammy. You can die, just like the rest of us."

"But I'm not like the rest of you! Not anymore."

"Yes, you are." Her voice is patient, the way I remember from my childhood when I would be all wound up in knots and acting out, and she would be so calm that, eventually, I would have no choice but to join her. "You always have been. Everything that happened on the outside didn't change who you are on the inside. I was afraid it might, but it hasn't." She lifts one hand from my shoulder and strokes my temple with the backs of her fingers.

"What am I supposed to do?" I whisper.

"You live your life."

"My *life?*" My jaw gapes as disbelief washes over me. I know my expression must look pretty intimidating, what with all the teeth, but Mom isn't fazed at all. "What kind of life can I possibly have?"

"The life you were meant to have."

"If this is what I was *meant* to have, maybe I don't want it. Have you thought of that?"

She tilts her head ever so slightly as she gazes at me. "I know, baby."

"Do you?" My teeth click. I'm starting to get angry, even though I know she's trying. She's trying to empathize. But I'm not sure even a mother could understand the life I've had to live for the last eleven years.

"I'm not going to tell you what to do, Sammy. That's up to you. The choices are yours, and I'll support them no matter what you decide."

"Like I have any choice," I mutter. "Even if I wanted out of this stupid life, I can't do anything about it. I'm stuck." My voice takes on a morose, whiny tone that I know Mom probably can't stand.

I can't stand it myself.

She gently taps my forehead with her index finger. "Think, Sammy. Think about what your body needs, what it can't do without. You can figure this out." Her expression is sad as she steps back. I long to follow her, but my feet seem to be rooted into the field. "Promise me, though, that that will be your last resort. Don't do anything you'll regret until you're sure the curse can't be broken. Don't give up your last chance before you even take it." She takes another step back, and the mist swirls between us, almost blocking her from my view. "Don't give up on the love that could save you."

I shake my head as she starts to disappear. I can't tell if the mist is swallowing her or if she's fading like the ghost she is.

"Mom? Don't go."

"I know you can do this. You can. Don't give up yet, all right?"

"Mom!" Her figure is hidden by the mist now. I struggle against the invisible bonds that hold me in place, and look down to see that they're not so invisible. The mist is colder now, sparkling as it flows around my limbs. I feel myself sink, like the ground is giving way. My limbs free themselves, and I reach out wildly as I slide into liquid darkness. Though my webbed toes suggest that I should be at home in the water, I can't coordinate my legs and arms, and my wings open uselessly, only to drag against the newfound resistance. "Mom!" I scream. "Don't leave me. Please, don't leave me. I love you. Come back! Come back . . ."

Water floods into my mouth as I wail in vain. My wings are heavy, useless weights that pull me down, and I can't seem to get my head above the surface again. Still, I fight, tearing at the water as if I could rend it limb from limb. As if it's my enemy.

And then, I can breathe.

I lie on my back, my wings pressed uncomfortably under me like a dried rose between the pages of a book. Gasping, I take stock of the blanket tangled around my aching legs and snagged in my toe claws, and the teddy in my hands, its neck gaping where its head has almost (but not quite) been ripped off.

"Mom." The word comes out in a tearless sob. I pull Fredo up against my face, turn over on my side, and curl up in a ball, tugging the blanket back over my exposed limbs.

As if I don't have enough to worry about, now I have to deal with my subconscious' mind games.

I press my nostrils against the bear's exposed neck fluff and squeeze my eyes shut, hoping that when I sleep again, it will be without dreams.

• 22 •

The Demon Debutante

Tegan returns two days later, and I've gone completely stir-crazy. Not only have I spent hours talking to the goats, I've also spent a worrying amount of time talking to myself. I made quick work of the rest of the angel book when I woke up the morning after my dream, and now I have no reading material.

Unless I want to read the book again.

Which I most definitely do not.

I'm ten feet up a tree, clinging to the bark, my body mostly hidden by the trunk, when I hear her enter the clearing. I go still.

"Sam?"

I spread my wings wide, and hear a startled swear.

"Don't do that! You scared the crap out of me." There's the sound of something heavy hitting the ground. "Besides . . . you could've given yourself away."

"To whom?" I ask. I slide down, sending flakes and curls of bark flying from under my claws. When my feet touch the solidity of the forest floor, I brush off my hands and emerge from behind the tree. Tegan stands next to a white plastic bag that seems to be bulging with something angular.

"I don't know. My dad. The police. Animal control."

"Do they know my name?"

"Oh. Good point." She watches as I grab my gloves from my small pile of borrowed belongings and slide them back on. "Hey! Fredo's still alive."

I glance at the bear, who's sitting on the folded blanket, his head listing precariously to one side. "Mostly."

She laughs. "I went to the library yesterday with Krissy. She now thinks I'm nuts, by the way." As she gestures to the bag at her feet, I realize that what's straining through the white plastic are the corners of books.

"How many did you get?"

"As many as I was allowed." She kneels down, even though the ground is damp, and reaches for the bag. Quickly, I unfurl the blanket and lay it out over the dirt and dead leaves. "Thanks. Okay, I wasn't sure what you wanted, so I got some of everything." She starts removing limp paperbacks and plastic-protected hardcovers from the bag, lining them up on the blanket as if she's a street vendor displaying her wares. "There's a couple of mysteries, a political thriller, some science fiction . . ." She pauses as she pulls another book from the bag and glances at my face. "This one's horror. You're not going to get too scared reading this out here by yourself in the deep, dark woods, are you?"

I snort with a squeak. She places the book down on the blanket, smiling wryly.

"I guess that's a no. Let's see . . ." She turns back to the bag, rummaging through the remaining books on the bottom. "I got you one trashy romance, just to cover all my bases. And there are a couple of classics in here, too. *Pride and Prejudice* and *Dracula*. Have you read either of those?"

"One of them."

"Oh. Well, I'm sure there's enough here that you can find something you haven't read." She slides *Dracula* back into the bag, assuming that's the one I've already read. I don't correct her.

"Thank you," I say.

"It was no problem. Just . . . don't eat any of these, okay? I'll have to pay fines if you do."

I nod solemnly. She starts to pack the rest of the books back into the bag.

"How was your weekend?" I ask. She shrugs, her shoulders creeping up toward her ears and then dropping away. It's a really exaggerated movement, and I have a feeling I've just asked a question that's going to have a troubling answer.

"Fine, I guess. I was kind of distracted, though. I was worrying about you."

"Me?"

"Yes, you, Sam. I didn't know what kind of trouble you'd get into. I was afraid you'd be seen, or Dad would come home from work early—"

"Does he do that often?"

"No. Not really. But I was just worrying about *everything,* you know? I guess I just would've rather spent the time here with you."

Well, that warms my heart. Just a little.

"It's not that I don't like hanging out with Krissy, because I do. I just . . . wasn't into it this time." She sighs and finishes putting the last book back into the bag, then sits back on her heels. "It's all good, though. I think Dad was relieved that I was doing stuff with my friends. He doesn't like it when I stay around here all the time." She grimaces. "Although, he is wondering why we're going through so many eggs. I had to make up some excuse about how I'm trying to get extra choline. Oh!" Her exclamation makes me twitch. "How are you doing for food? You must be starving."

"I could eat."

"I'm sure. Wait here," she says, getting to her feet. "I'll go grab something for you."

When she returns a few minutes later, she's got a whole carton of eggs in one hand, her tablet in the other. She passes me the carton and sits cross-legged on the blanket.

"Eat. And then there's something I need to show you."

"What?" The suspiciousness is so audible in my voice that she shakes her head with a smile.

"It's nothing bad. At least, I don't think it's bad. Anyway, eat first. Then I'll show you. I can hear your stomach from here."

I open the carton—it's full—and quickly eat four of the eggs. After closing it back up, I set it next to Fredo, who's sitting on the angel book. His head is really cocked to the side now; he looks like he's fascinated by something.

"What did you want to show me?" I ask.

"Sit." She pats the blanket next to her. I obey, feeling a bit like a trained dog. As she turns on the tablet and starts to search for something, I study her face until her hair falls in a curtain over her cheek, obscuring her features. She tucks it behind her ear impatiently and angles the screen toward me.

"What?" I ask.

"I thought you could read."

I click my teeth once in agitation and peer at the screen. But before I can really read anything, she's talking again.

"I was thinking about you, and how you're the only one of your kind. I mean, that can't possibly be true. You had to come from somewhere. So there have to be others. I searched—plugging in your features: your wings, your tail, stuff like that—and found this. What do you think?"

I haven't even had a chance to read it yet. Leaning closer, I look at the page she's brought up. It's some sort of biography.

"Delilah Warren," I say, reading the name out loud. Her year of birth is given as 1927. There's no date of death.

"She was a circus freak," Tegan says. "That sounds so awful . . . but that's what they called them back then. And Delilah Warren was . . . well, she was known as the Demon Debutante."

"The *what?*"

Tegan swipes her finger upward, scrolling the page. When it comes to a stop on an old, hand-tinted photograph, I suck in a gasp. "See?" she says triumphantly. "I knew you weren't the only one."

I grab the tablet from her and stare at the photo. The

figure is small and delicate, dressed in a long, ruffled gown that reaches the floor. The dress is dark, nearly the same colour as the woman's skin. Were it not for the dress, I might have been looking at a photo of myself. The woman has neither nose nor ears, and her lower face is split by a wide grin of obsidian teeth. Her wings are open in a dramatic spread, and her elongated, clawed fingers are adorned with sparkling rings set with dark gems.

"Holy crap," I whisper.

"She was apparently part of some circus show back in the forties. Toured with them for a while. Nobody really knew what was going on with her. Critics thought it was all fake. Makeup and costuming. A really impressive mask. But I think she might've been like you, Sam."

I'm having a hard time breathing. I stare at the woman's face in wonder. I thought I was the only one. Obviously, I'm not. Or . . . I wasn't.

"What happened to her?" I ask. "Is she still alive?"

"That's the weird thing," Tegan says, taking the tablet back from me and scrolling to the end of the biography. "Nobody knows. Here. It says that in nineteen forty-five she suddenly disappeared, at the same time as one of the other freaks. Some guy named Len Merrill. He was tattooed from head to toe. Pretty creepy." She angles the tablet to show me the picture. Mr. Merrill looks like a pretty ordinary human being to me, albeit highly embellished.

"You think *he's* the creepy one?"

She ignores my comment. "He rejoined the circus a few years after that, but Delilah was never seen again. That's pretty weird, don't you think?"

"Why?"

"Because she'd be noticeable. If she was like you, she wouldn't have been able to go anywhere without drawing attention. I don't know." She gives a little shrug. "Maybe she went into hiding. Maybe she died. The point, Sam, is that you're not the only one. There are others like you out there. Or, there were, back in the forties."

I'm not sure how this is supposed to make me feel. Better? Less alone? Comforted by the fact that I'm not the only one who's had to deal with this stupid curse?

Tegan scrolls back up to the top of the page, and another picture flickers past. I reach out and grab her wrist, my gloved fingers closing around it. She looks up, startled.

"Stop. Go back."

"To what?"

"Just . . . there," I say when the picture rolls back into view again. "What is that?"

"It's the emblem for the circus Delilah and Len worked for. It says here that all the performers had it tattooed somewhere on their bodies. Talk about being loyal to your boss." She shakes her head. "Why?"

The black eagle, its wings spread wide, is so familiar. It tickles the edges of my consciousness, irritating my brain with something just out of reach.

"Have you seen it somewhere before, Sam?"

The realization hits me like a blow to the solar plexus. Yes, I've seen it before. At the time, though, I didn't know what it was. But now, as I stare at the black eagle, the image overlays itself on an old memory of a smudgy black mark on an old woman's wrist. I thought it was a bat. A bat to go with an old witch.

I swallow the vomit I can feel rising up the back of my throat. Delilah Warren. Adelijda Woroniecki. Tegan's words replay themselves in my head: *"I pity someone who hurts other people, because they only do that if they've been hurt themselves."*

Though the revelation brings up more new questions than it answers, I feel a surge of warm hope shoot through me. Because now I know this: The curse can be broken. Aunt Adelijda broke it all those years ago. And if a horrible woman like that could do it, maybe I can, too. It's possible. It's not probable, but it's possible. I let out a soft chirp (I just can't help myself) and stand up. My wings tremble with excitement as I start to pace around the clearing.

Tegan looks up at me from the blanket. "Pretty cool, eh? I mean, at least we know now that you're not the only one."

Oh, but we know so much more than that. I want to tell her, but . . . My feet skid to a stop, scuffing in the dead pine needles. Is she supposed to know? What if there are terms of the curse nobody ever told me about? What if telling her the truth nullifies something, and her love—on the remote chance she might ever grow to love me—won't be enough anymore? What if any love she might have for me turns into pity when she finds out I'm a cursed human and not the cryptozoological oddity she thinks I am? My heart aches and itches with the need to say it. To tell her what I am and what happened to me. What must have happened to Aunt Adelijda, too.

But I can't. I know I can't. The risk is just too great. My wings sag.

"It's too bad we couldn't find any more recent examples," Tegan says, absently flicking her fingers up and down the screen. "I looked, but this was the only article I could find." She sighs and closes the browser app. "Anyway. I just thought you'd want to know."

"Thank you." My body is rigid, tense. The elation of just a few moments earlier is gone.

"No problem. Looking that stuff up gave me an excuse to procrastinate about my calculus homework." She sticks her tongue out in disgust. "I always liked math, but this . . . I don't think it's actually math. It's *evil*."

In spite of my lingering disappointment, I can't help releasing an amused snort.

"Are you mocking my pain?" She sticks out her bottom lip in an exaggerated pout.

"Of course not. I'm empathizing."

"You're familiar with calculus?"

"I *was*. It's been a few years, but I can probably remember some of it."

She just stares at me. I shrink back, suddenly feeling awkward.

"What?"

"Calculus, Sam? Seriously?"

"It's not that hard."

She blows out a breath, sending the wisps of hair around her face trembling. "One of these days, Sam, you and I are going to have a long talk about all these *surprises* of yours."

"One day," I say.

One day, I promise myself, *I'll tell her everything.*

• 23 •

Animal Control

"Like this?" Tegan asks as she jots down the numbers with a pencil. Before she can even finish, I see the mistake she's made. I shake my head.

"No. You need to factor in the second variable."

She makes a disgusted sort of noise and scratches out her work. "I'm never going to get this."

"Sure you are. I'm an excellent teacher."

"Who else have you taught?"

"Nobody." When she shakes her head with a smile, I click my teeth at her. "But I know how to motivate my students."

"Yeah . . . somehow, Sam, I don't think that fear is a great motivator for calculus." She stares at the problem for a few more seconds, her pencil poised above the notebook. Then she drops her forehead onto it with a deep sigh. We're stretched out on our stomachs on the blanket. When we started, I made sure to keep my wings tightly furled against my back. But now that I've relaxed, they have, too, and are sort of spread out. My right wing is lying across Tegan's back. She hasn't mentioned it, and I'm in no hurry to move it; the warmth of her body against the thin membrane feels good.

"You're not afraid of me." I hold my breath, afraid she'll deny it.

"No." Her voice is muffled. "I guess that's why I still suck at calculus." Finally raising her head, she looks at me. The spiral along the top edge of her notebook has left a faint impression on her forehead. "You need to be scarier."

I'm not quite sure how to do that. I mean, I thought I had the nightmare thing down already. Asking me to be scarier is like . . . I don't know . . . asking a chicken to be more tasty.

"Try harder," she says.

"I don't need to try. Look at me."

She shrugs and turns back to the page. "I'm used to it. You're going to have to up your game, buddy, if you really want to motivate me."

The thought occurs to me that I could try to kiss her. I'm sure the sight of my teeth coming at her face would give her all the motivation she could ever need. A sad chuckle escapes through my nostrils.

"What's so funny?"

"Nothing." It's the truth. I adjust my elbows on the blanket and trace one gloved finger over the gaudy geometric pattern. Tegan slides her pencil into the notebook's spiral and pushes both away from her as she falls onto her side and looks up at me.

"You've been . . . I don't know." Her forehead creases into

a frown, and her dark eyes look sad. "Since the weekend, you've been different. Did something happen?"

Aside from my dead mother visiting me in a dream with obscure hints on how to end my miserable existence? No. Nothing at all. I look down and see her hair spilled across the blanket, coming within inches of my hand. My fingers long to feel it, but I hold them back; with the gloves on, it's pointless, anyway.

"Sam, I know you're lonely, but I—" She breaks off suddenly and sits up, pushing against my wing that's draped over her side. I glance up just in time—and too late—as the sound of the footsteps that alerted her suddenly register in my own mind.

Crap.

"Mija." Tegan's father stands just feet away, his bleary eyes wide. His hair is sticking up on one side, like he just got out of bed, and the worn bathrobe he's hugging closed only adds to that impression. He doesn't look at me. It's as if he can't; he knows I'm here, but something prevents him from fully turning his gaze on me and really taking me in. He probably knows that, if he does, he'll never be able to get the sight out of his head.

"Dad. What . . ." She licks her lips, for once at a loss for words. "What do you want?"

"What are you doing?" His voice is breathy. The belt of his robe hangs loose, and I can see the ends trembling along with his body. Slowly, I push myself up to my knees. He rushes forward and grabs Tegan by the arm, half hauling, half dragging her to her feet. She lets out a cry.

"Dad, stop! It's all right. He's—"

"Chupacabra," he says. "El diablo. It should be dead." He takes a step back, pulling Tegan with him. "It's unnatural." He whirls her around to face him, and his knuckles are white as he grasps her upper arms. "What are you doing?"

"He's my friend, Dad. His name is Sam. And he's not a chupacabra. Or a devil. We're not sure what he is, but—"

"Are you listening to yourself, mija? Look at it. Look." He spins her around to face me. I slowly get to my feet, trying to look as unthreatening as possible and failing miserably. My back is hunched like I'm going to spring, and my teeth are bared in preparation for biting. At least, I'm sure that's what it looks like to him. Tegan stares at me, making the direct eye contact that her father, so far, hasn't. Her lower lip quivers.

"I am looking."

Her father swears and turns her away from me. "It's gotten into your head. Seduced you. That's what they do to lure their prey."

He thinks I *seduced* her? He actually thinks I could?

"Go and get the gun." His whisper is loud, and if he intended for me not to hear him, he failed. Tegan shakes her head.

"No. Dad, just stop and listen for a moment. If you'd just talk to him—"

"One of us needs to keep our wits about us," he says, his voice rising. "I'm not going to give that thing the opportunity to lure me into its web of trickery. It wants something, and it's using you to get it."

A little gasp escapes my throat as the truth of his words hits me. I take a step back. A skeletal leaf crunches softly under my foot, and her father looks up. His gaze is point-edly low, focusing on my exposed genitals.

"Did it touch you, mija? Did it try to . . . Did you let it . . ." His voice is choked, and he can't even bring himself to voice the horrible thought that hangs in the air of the clearing. Tegan tears herself away from him, but she doesn't move in my direction. That's probably a wise choice.

"No! Dad. Don't be stupid."

My gaze drops to the ground, and I feel my wings sag.

"Sam. I'm sorry. I didn't mean it that way."

"It's all right." It's true. It *is* stupid. It's a stupid thought, a stupid hope.

"No, it's not all right." She squares her shoulders and faces down her father. "He's my friend, Dad. That's all. And even if it was more than that, you have no right to come out here and accuse him of—"

"It's a demon. A devil. I'm just trying to protect you, mija."

"I don't need protecting! Not from Sam."

"Stop." He closes his eyes and shakes his head. "Don't use its name. You're strengthening your bond with it."

"Oh, for god's sake, Dad." She fixes her father with a fiery stare. I'm glad I'm not on the receiving end of it. "Don't believe everything you read. Sam is not evil. And, yes, I have a bond with him. That's a *good* thing. He's not manipulating me. He's not using me. He doesn't want anything from me."

"Tegan," I begin, but when she looks over at me, my mouth locks up and I can't remember what it was I wanted to say. My jaws snap together, sending my teeth clicking.

Her father lets out a little cry, followed by a string of curses, and grabs her arm once more.

"The gun. Go and get the gun."

"You go get it, if you want it so badly!" Her shout sounds like it's on the verge of tears. She wrenches free and stares him down. Her nostrils flare as she stands there, breathing hard, her fists clenched at her sides. "Go ahead and shoot him. But if you do, I'll hate you for it. If you kill my friend, I'll never forgive you."

"It's in your head, mija." He points at her forehead, his finger trembling. "It's gotten in your head. You don't understand. It's dangerous. Do you have any idea what it will do to you?"

"Nothing!" she shouts. "Sam would never hurt me. You only think he will because you don't know him!"

Her father stands there for a moment longer before I see the change in his expression. The resolve hits all at once, and I know he's just decided what he needs to do: He needs to protect his daughter. And there's only one way to do that. As he turns and runs back to the house, his robe flapping around his knees, Tegan lets out a sob and turns to me.

"You have to go. Now."

I don't move. My gaze drifts down to the blanket, then over to Fredo and the bag of books. I'm so tired all of a sudden. My feet step forward, onto the blanket. I fall into a crouch and hug my knees.

"No. Sam, get up." She falls to her knees in front of me. "Get up, now. When he comes back here, he's going to shoot you."

"I know."

"So you're going to make it easy for him? Sam, he knows you're not easy to kill. He's not stupid. He's going to aim for your head this time. I know you said you heal quickly, but do you really think you can heal from that?"

"We're going to find out."

"Damn it, Sam!"

Her fist catches me on the left temple. The blow is so unexpected that, for a moment, I lose my balance. My wings unfurl, and I fall heavily onto my ass, crushing my tail beneath me.

"Go!" she screams. "I don't want to watch you get your head blown off. Why would you do that to me, Sam? Why?" She's crying now, greyish trails running down her cheeks as her mascara releases itself from her eyelashes. "Please, Sam. Please." She curls over so far that the ends of her hair brush the blanket. "Please . . ."

"Where am I supposed to go?"

"Anywhere," she whispers. "Anywhere but here." She looks up. A blink releases another cascade of tears. "Just get as far away from here as you can."

I stand and pull my wings tightly against my back. For a moment, I just stand there, staring down at her kneeling form. The memory of the damage from the first gunshot works its way into my head. Flayed flesh. The sickly smell of my own blood. And I know I can't do this to her. If her father does the same thing to my head . . . I don't want her to have to see that. Even if such a thing would mean my own freedom.

So I go. I walk into the trees. Then I run. I pass behind the barn, saying a silent goodbye to Letitia and Fergus. I pump my legs hard and keep my wings tightly furled, trying to stay as aerodynamic as possible as I bolt through the sunlit field. Back to the park. Back to the quiet woods, where I can be a shadow. A lonely shadow. A cursed shadow.

When I reach the stream on the far side of the light blue trail, I fall to my knees beside it. My breath comes in sharp pants. I realize I've just lost everything, and yet I'm too numb to even care. A twig digs into my knee. The creek chills the tip of my wing to a painful cold. My fists are clenched so tightly that my fingers might break.

None of it matters. It's over. It doesn't matter how long I have left until my birthday. I know it's not long enough.

Maybe it never was.

I let myself slump sideways, into the trickle of water. My muscles tighten at the shock of the temperature, then go slack as I sink into the cold comfort of the stream. It rushes over my head, then tries to go up my nostrils. I cough, sputtering, unable to breathe. Instinctively, my body rears up, away from the prospect of drowning.

"Mom," I whisper as the stinging sensation in my sinuses gives way to the realization. She told me to think about what my body needs. What it can't live without.

Air. It can't live without air.

The stream won't be enough. Not when I can so easily pull myself out of it. A backyard pool probably won't work, either. Besides . . . who wants to find *me* stuck in their pool filter? No. I need a bigger body of water. An ocean. A river. A lake.

As I pull myself out of the frigid stream and shake the water from my body, it's with a strange sense of relief. Now

I know that, after November first, I won't be trapped. I have a way out, should I need to use it.

It certainly looks like I'm going to need it, too.

I collapse against a nearby tree and pull my knees to my chest. A weird mixture of grief and hope flows through me. It's both hot and cold, and my body isn't sure whether to shiver or go limp. In the end, it compromises by falling into a light sleep that refuses to deepen into anything remotely restful or refreshing. But I'm just as glad for that. I don't think I could bear dreaming about Tegan right now . . . and I'm pretty sure that, with everything that's just happened, I would.

• 24 •

I Forgot to File a Flight Plan

After the sun goes down, I walk back to the edge of the park and stare out over the field. I can just make out the lights from Tegan's house glittering between the trees. One of the windows upstairs is lit. I wonder if that's her room. I imagine her sitting at her desk, continuing to struggle over her calculus homework. Although, she was pretty upset when I left; calculus is probably not at the top of her list of things to do right now, even though the difficulty would take her mind off what happened this afternoon.

I should've known something like that would happen. Fate has something else in store for me, apparently. Something monstrous and eternal. I stare up at the sky, but it's clouded over and there's not a star to be seen. A nipping wind races across the field, and if I had even one solitary hair anywhere on my body, I'm sure it would be standing on end.

It seems that Aunt Adelijda made the most of her curse.

She made a living from it, anyway. What have I done? Sat in a hospital basement for eleven years, letting other people feed me. I even let Tegan feed me. A low growl escapes my throat as I think about it. I'm so useless. What's the point of being in a body like this—claws and teeth and all—if I don't even use it to my advantage?

Well, we all know how that turned out. I have no desire to go back to stealing chickens, even though I know I'm going to have to. Maybe not here, though. I should probably move on and take up "hunting" in a neighbourhood where the neighbours aren't already on guard against a chupacabra.

Or whatever it is the rest of them think I am.

I take a step farther into the field. The wind whispers through the weeds, sending them rustling. It sounds like there might be a million rats scurrying around me. It would be awesome if that were true; I'm feeling a little peckish.

I spread my wings and listen as the breeze gently pulls against the membranes with a fluttering sound. It feels good to stretch them wide, and the tension in my shoulders that I've carried for hours begins to ease.

I see the gust of wind before I feel it, racing toward me on swaying weeds. A moment later, my toes leave the ground as the wind buffets me back, catching my wings like a kite. I suck in a gasp of surprise and flap hard. My toes hover for a second longer before returning to the ground.

No way.

I crouch low (knowing I'm going to feel awfully silly if this doesn't work) and launch myself up into the wind again, flapping my wings as hard as I can. This time, I rise about ten feet into the air before crashing to the ground, jarring my newly healed ankles.

As I suspected, weeks ago when I broke it, my bent right wing is proving to be a bit of a problem. But since I really have no desire to spend the night regrowing a new one, I resolve to find a way to compensate. Birds fly with crookedly healed wings all the time. Why should I be any different?

I crouch down and spring into the air once more. This time, I try to hold back a little on the left. The short flight is cleaner than the previous one, and I land, awkwardly, a few feet away.

I can't believe it. Am I actually flying? Maybe it's all just a dream. Kneeling in the weeds, I nip at my arm with my teeth. The sharp pain, delayed only a fraction of a second as the nerves scream their signals to my brain, makes me growl.

So. Not a dream.

Pushing to my feet, I sprint across the field toward Tegan's house. When I've built up enough speed—or, at least, what I *hope* is enough speed—I open my wings and feel the air press into them. I pull hard against the air, and am caught in a sudden swoop. A laugh bursts out of me as my feet leave the ground, and I climb up, my flight path a para- bolic curve over the treetops. I look down, seeing the dark field, the even-darker trees. The barn's roof is a featureless expanse of grey. I pass over Tegan's house and look out across the landscape. I can see the road, the farms beyond. The woods where I turned into a monster—I mean, even more than I already was—crouch in the distance. I have no desire to go back there, so I turn my head to the left and angle my body in the direction I want to go.

The turn costs me a bit of altitude, so I flap hard. The ground recedes below me once more as I sail out over the field beside Tegan's house. I make a wide loop, flapping my wings whenever I get too low, but mostly just letting them carry me on the wind. After a few more minutes, I start to feel the ache in my shoulders. What did I expect? It's not like I've done much with those muscles for the past eleven years. I suppose it's time to land.

A burst of panic hits me as I realize I'm not quite sure how to do that.

Well, what's the worst that can happen? I break a wing? Been there. I break a leg? Done that. I make a complete fool of myself in front of all the other nocturnal creatures? I can handle a few laughing raccoons.

I head back toward the expanse of field closest to the park before I make my first landing attempt. I'm not quite sure how to slow down or stop, so I figure it'll have to be a running landing. After a couple of large, circular passes to lower my altitude, my toes are only about three feet off the ground, my claws catching on the weeds. I grit my teeth and hold my arms out in front of myself. A couple more flaps drop me toward the ground. My already-running feet meet the dirt. Now I just need to stop.

But momentum has other ideas.

I crash, face first, into the weeds in what is probably the most ungraceful landing ever made by a winged creature. I can feel my wings flail and flap as I come to a skidding stop on my stomach. There's dirt in my teeth. There's a twig in my nostril. But I'm in one piece. I spring to my feet, letting out a series of elated chirps and doing what—to anyone watching—probably looks like the equivalent of a really bad end zone dance. But I don't care if anyone's watching. I brush the dust from my knees before practically skipping back into the park. I might feel it in my wings tomorrow, but it was totally worth it.

I'm going to sleep well tonight.

• 25 •

Parking-Lot Sushi

I should've grabbed the carton of eggs when I ran away, but I didn't, and now I'm famished. As the sun rises, my stomach complains. Loudly. I hope the hardcore hikers have crappy hearing.

It takes me a couple of hours to make my way to the entrance of the park. I walk parallel to the trails, staying as far into the woods as I can while still being able to see the route markers that are nailed, at intervals, to the trees. There isn't as much undergrowth as there was even a few weeks ago, so I'm able to see the humans in their brightly coloured jackets long before they're able to see me, allowing me to duck behind a tree or under a fallen log until they pass. The only close call comes when someone lets their dog off its leash, and it comes bounding up to me, tail wagging. I stare at the dumbest dog in the world in disbelief before clicking my teeth at it. It bounds a few feet away, then turns back to me, tongue dangling from its mouth.

"Go away."

Its tongue disappears as it closes its mouth, and it stares at me, head cocked to the side in a posture that reminds me of Fredo. I press myself back against a nearby tree and try not to encourage it. Finally, its owners call for it, and, with a last glance at me, it bounds off toward the path.

The trees thin out a bit before the parking lot, which allows me to see that it's almost deserted. There are about half a dozen cars there, ranging from a sporty little hybrid to a massive SUV with an out-of-province vanity plate that reads CHSGR8R. Choose greater? Cheese grater? It's impossible to tell whether the owner is a motivational speaker or a chef. In any case, they're smart enough to have locked their doors. I slink between the vehicles, testing each door handle, checking every window for a gap I might be able to wiggle my fingers into. I'm not sure what I'm looking for. The chances of finding anything I can eat are pretty remote.

The first unlocked door belongs to a little red car that reminds me of the one that almost ran me over during my escape from the hospital. I pull open the door and climb inside. It smells sort of floral, but not in a natural way. A faded air-freshener dangles from the rearview mirror.

I may never have gotten my licence or learned to drive—actually, I haven't even been in a car for almost eleven years—but I've made it a point to learn all I can. So I know where to find the latch that opens the trunk. I get out and, still crouching, make my way to the back of the car. The trunk turns out to be empty. Really empty. The place where the spare tire should be is just a gaping depression.

After closing the trunk and the front door of the red car, I move on. All of the remaining vehicles are locked up tight . . . except for the little white hybrid that's parked right beside the trailhead. Through the back window, I can see a plastic cooler sitting on the floor behind the passenger seat. I tell myself it's probably empty. Either that, or it's full of beer. Or smoked ham. Or potato salad. Or something else that sounds like it should be appetizing, but isn't. I flick the door lock button, then scramble into the back seat.

The cooler isn't empty. In fact, it's quite full. I suppose somebody is planning a picnic for after their walk. Too bad for them. They should've kept their doors locked.

I pull away the plastic bag of pre-cut raw veggies and toss it on the seat. It's quickly followed by some PB&Js on white bread. I wouldn't want to eat those even if I were human. (I never did like white bread.) At the bottom of the cooler, nestled against four ice-cold cans of pop, are two plastic clamshell packages. I almost ignore them . . . and then I register what they are. It *might* work . . .

I remove the clamshells and place them carefully on the seat while I repack the rest of the food and close the cooler. Then I take my prize and escape back into the woods. The owners of the hybrid are going to be pretty confused when they return from their walk. I mean, who breaks into a car to steal pre-packaged sushi?

Staying as close as I can to the trailhead, I find a spot where I can enjoy my snack. That's all it is, really. The seaweed and rice is completely unappetizing, so I remove my gloves and use my claws to carefully pluck the pieces of raw tuna and salmon from the rolls. It's palatable, but only barely; I have a feeling I would enjoy it a lot more if the fish were actually alive and squirming in my jaws. But beggars can't be choosers.

And I'm definitely a beggar.

When I've extracted all the edible food I can, I place the hollowed-out sushi rolls back in the packages with the untouched ginger and wasabi. I do feel sort of bad for wasting the rest, but there's not much I can do about that. I think about returning what's left to the cooler, but that's an awfully big risk to take for a bit of rice and seaweed. So I crawl through the bushes to the edge of the path and slide the packages onto the hard-packed earth where the next hiker is sure to see them. I know nobody's going to eat mystery food that appears on the side of a hiking trail, but I don't know what else to do with it.

All of that effort, and my stomach is still near empty.

I'll have to come up with another plan.

When the sun goes down, the rain that's been threatening all day begins in earnest. I shake the water from my wings as I emerge into the field. I don't mind the rain. In fact, it's probably a good thing. Rain means clouds, which means there's no clear moon to be silhouetted against as I fly.

And fly I do. I shoot out over the field, keeping low at first, practising holding my legs up so my toes don't brush the weeds below. The force of my wings sends the wet foliage bending away from me, droplets spraying. I'm grateful for the cover of darkness provided by the rain-clouds, though not so enthused as I start to feel heavy and swollen with water. I decide to cut my practice short so I can slink back to my new home in the park and curl up under my wings to wait out the showers.

The next morning, all that remains of the rain are the intermittent drips from the upper branches splashing onto the forest floor. They splash onto me, too, onto my droplet-beaded head and waterlogged wings. I spend the morning walking through the trees with my wings spread wide in an attempt to dry them out. I wonder if flying will help speed up the process, but when I try to leap into the air, aiming my body for a branch twenty feet above my head, I find I can't go anywhere. It's like I've got two sodden sponges strapped to my shoulders. Annoyed, I flap my wings hard. But it's no use. I just need to wait to dry out.

I realize that I never did get a chance to ask Tegan the date. The thought occurs to me that I might already be eighteen. The curse might already be permanent. Would I have felt something? I mean, if you've got this curse that's going to keep you trapped in the form of a nightmare for all eternity, you would think you'd feel *something*. I don't know what, exactly. Maybe nausea. Or a sudden headache. You might feel a jolt through your body. Or maybe just a little spark on the tip of your nose . . . or where your nose used to be.

Surprisingly, the thought that my fate might already be

sealed doesn't bother me as much as I thought it would. I expected wailing and gnashing of teeth. Unbearable grief. Hopeless heartache.

Maybe I was just being overly dramatic in my imaginings.

No . . . I'm almost at peace with it. I guess learning to fly has taken some of the sting out of this existence of mine. It *is* pretty cool. I mean, of course I would give it up in a heartbeat if I could go back to being human again, but . . . if you have to be trapped in the body of a monster forever, there are worse things than being able to fly.

I wonder if Aunt Adelijda ever learned to fly. She obviously knew what our claws could do. But what about the rest? Did she struggle with getting enough to eat? Did she ever learn to use her wings as anything more than a fancy decoration?

I have no idea how she broke the curse, but I suspect it had something to do with Len Merrill. Maybe he was able to see past her monstrous appearance long enough to fall in love. After that . . . I don't know. I have a sneaking suspicion that there was no happily ever after for Aunt Adelijda. Maybe that's why she turned her anger—and the curse—on me.

Back beside my stream, I crouch down, out of reach of any of the drips falling from above, and continue to think. I wonder about who cursed Aunt Adelijda. Was it someone who had been cursed themselves? Is that how this works? If I had broken the curse, would I have been able to pass it along to someone else, the way Aunt Adelijda did with me?

I don't know. And there's nobody to ask. Nobody ever told me as much, but I know that Aunt Adelijda—the only person who might've been able to answer my questions—

is dead, indirectly killed by her own cruelty toward me. I remember the four red lines appearing on her papery, weathered cheek like invisible ink slowly being revealed. My poison killed her . . . and, with her, my chances at understanding.

I suppose it doesn't really matter. Even if I *did* know how to pass on the curse to someone else, I wouldn't want to. I can't think of anything more cruel to do to another person than to isolate them, turn them into an object of revulsion, and ensure they'll spend the rest of their life lonely and alone. Would I have passed it back to Aunt Adelijda if given the chance? No, I don't think I would have done that, either. Even after what she did to me, I don't think I could've retaliated that way. Not when I knew what I would've been inflicting on her.

I wonder if she's laughing at me. Thinking I'm soft for not wanting to strike back at her. Amusing herself with the thought of my eternal fate.

I don't care.

I stand up and stretch my wings wide. "I don't care," I say aloud. "You thought you could destroy me with this. But you didn't. You thought your hatred and cruelty would turn me into a monster. And maybe that's what I look like. Maybe that's what everybody sees. But that's *not* what I am." My fists clench in their gloves until I can hear the leather strain against my knuckles. "My name is Sam Woroniecki, and I am a human being. You can't take that away from me, no matter what you did, no matter how you made me look. I am human, and I always will be. You did *not* win."

As soon as I stop speaking, the silence is almost complete, cut through only by the steady trickling of the stream. My breath escapes in a long, whistling sigh, and I fold my wings tightly against my back, suddenly aware of the irony of declaring myself human while standing under my own pair of functional wings. I feel the skin around my mouth tighten in a smile that only I know is there.

Somehow, I think Aunt Adelijda would appreciate that irony.

The sky is still dark with clouds when I emerge into the field that night, but the rain stays suspended above. I practise taking off, jumping straight up, and then perching in one of the nearby trees before leaping out into the open and gliding back to the ground. My landings are much softer than that first one, when Tegan dared me to jump out of the tree.

I miss her. I miss her so much it hurts, and though I'm not really scared of her father over what he might do to me, I don't like the idea of what seeing him hurt me would do to her. So I keep my distance, purposely staying far away from the stand of trees that surrounds their house and barn.

After about ten near-perfect takeoffs and landings, I take to the air in earnest, pumping my wings hard to gain as much altitude as I can. Since I'm not afraid of heights, I push harder, until I find myself blowing through the low-hanging clouds, a dark shadow flying through the night. I catch glimpses of the ground far below, houses like tiny models that don't look big enough to hold a person, let alone a whole family and their lives. My wings grow a bit sluggish as the water collects on my skin, so I dip lower until I'm in the clear air once more.

The night sparkles with lights, mostly in shades of yellow and white: the headlights of cars, street lights, porch lights . . . even somebody's pool, lit up in blue. I shudder at the thought of swimming in November. Or December. It's going to be pretty up here in another month or so, once all the Christmas lights are on display. I haven't seen them in person for years. Well, except for the pathetic string of multicoloured lights Dr. Grant brought out to decorate my doorway every year. But they were nothing compared to the displays I saw on TV, that I was never allowed to go out and see for myself.

This year will be different, though. This year, I can go wherever I want and see whatever I want to see.

The air is full of water droplets that mist against my skin and eyeballs as I soar through the night, carried by my strengthening wings. I can't see them that well, but I think they might actually be a bit bigger. Bulkier. My muscles are getting stronger, in any case. If my right wing weren't crooked, I might actually be able to fly to Cancun, liked I joked about with Tegan.

Well, maybe not. I'm not sure I'd make it through American airspace unscathed.

After an hour or so, I turn back the way I came. It's a good thing I thought to follow one of the major roads, or I might never find my way back. I think the return trip is a little quicker; the wind feels like it's behind me, pushing me along, urging me back home. At one point, I spread my arms and legs and toes wide, and close my eyes for a moment, letting the cold air whisper through all my nooks and crannies, and just enjoy the sensation of weightlessness as I fly. It's quiet up here, except for the whistle of wind past my earholes and the gentle flap of my wing membranes. It's peaceful. At last, I open my eyes and reorient myself, adjusting my course back toward the road.

As I approach Tegan's property once more, my heart hitches. I wish I could show her. Maybe, one day, I will. I don't think she ever believed I couldn't fly. And, wouldn't you know it? She was right. I have a feeling I'm in for a big "I told you so" when I show her what I can do . . . but I don't think I'll mind.

I swoop low over the fields beside her house, turning my head as I race past. The lights are off, and I can't see anything in the darkened windows. She's probably sound asleep, dreaming of . . . whatever teenage girls dream of.

Judging by the books she likes to read, probably handsome young men with supernatural powers.

I make my most graceful landing yet just outside the park and continue to walk in a smooth motion, not missing a beat. I've got the hang of it now. It seems amazing I ever plummeted out of that tree in the first place.

• 26 •

No, Thanks ... I'm Allergic

The next morning, as I skulk through the trees on my daily walk around the park, a rustling in the undergrowth makes me stop short. It's nothing big—I can tell that much from the sound—but I still find my muscles tensing and bunching, preparing me for flight. On my feet or wings, whichever feels like the better option. It seems I haven't quite gotten used to the fact that I'm likely to be the more dangerous party in any encounter.

I step forward and push aside a clutch of withered ferns. A smallish bird stares back at me with one beady eye. Its black plumage is inky in the shadows, but even so, I can see the bent wing and broken feathers. It goes still for a moment when it sees me, and then it goes nuts. Can I blame it?

"It's all right," I say, trying to make my voice soft and soothing as I reach for the flailing creature. As I pick it up in my gloved hands, it takes a swipe at me with its beak. I give a surprised click of my teeth as the sharp point cuts across my forearm. "I'm just trying to help," I say, a little less patient now. The bird lets out a plaintive cry, like a toy that's winding down.

I'm no vet. I have no idea how to fix a bird's wing. Heck, I couldn't even fix my own properly. At least I can fly, though; I can't say the same for this poor creature. It stares up at me, its beady little eyes twitching and rolling in fear.

I *could* put it out of its misery. That would be the kind thing to do. That's what I tell myself, anyway. But I find that, as I hold the warm little body in my hands, I can't. I feel a sort of affinity with this black bird. We're both alone out here, broken to varying degrees. My stomach growls with impatience, but I ignore it.

Instead of eating the bird—as I would've done just a few days ago—I carry it back to my home near the stream. When I place it in my new nest, it flails around a little, then goes still. I stand up and stare down at it, my guts roiling with conflict.

I know I could eat it. I know I probably should. If I'm going to survive, I'm going to need to eat something. But . . . not this.

I never knew I could eat eggs until Tegan offered me some. I never knew I could eat raw fish, either, until I dismantled those sushi rolls. Now I wonder if I've spent eleven years eating live creatures—swallowing rats' heads and biting the wings off of chickens—when I didn't really need to. Sure, I enjoyed it on some level (I'm not going to deny it), but maybe it wasn't necessary. The thought that

Dr. Grant could've just brought me a raw chicken leg or a piece of steak, wrapped in plastic and far removed from the actual killing, fills me with a sudden anger. Did he enjoy watching me kill my meals? He viewed me as a monster and assumed I needed to eat like one. But maybe I didn't. I might not have enjoyed eating pre-butchered raw meat, but I didn't enjoy eating broccoli before the transformation, either. That doesn't mean it didn't nourish my body.

As the bird continues to make pathetic little noises, I take a step back. I won't eat it. I don't know what I'm going to eat, but I know it's not the creature in front of me.

I turn and head off into the trees.

When I return an hour or so later, a tasting menu of various bugs and worms in the palm of one hand, the bird is gone. Most of it, anyway. A few black feathers lie next to a pair of little bird feet. Blood stains the leaves of the nest. I let the bird food fall from my hand and turn away.

It looks like I'm not the only predator in the park.

While a part of me feels bad for leaving the bird there, helpless and vulnerable, another part of me can't help but feel a little bit relieved.

I'm less of a beast than whatever else lurks in these woods.

My flight this evening is another long one. I head down the road that Tegan's house is on, then turn left on a corner with a huge, sprawling willow. The sky is still dreary and dark, and there's not too much wind. It's perfect flying weather. A few more weeks and I'll probably freeze my tail off, but, for now, the temperature isn't too unbearable.

I stay well away from the road and keep to the backs of the large properties, hoping that nobody bothers to glance out their windows. The houses get larger as I go. Some are set back from the street at the ends of lit driveways, the windows dark.

I fly on into the night.

It isn't long before the land falls away and there's nothing but an inky, featureless expanse below me. I'm confused for a moment, since I know Tegan's house isn't anywhere near the ocean. When I see faint lights glimmering on the far side, I realize I'm flying above a lake.

Wasn't this what I wanted to find? My ideation of just a few days ago seems like the overly dramatic plan of a defeatist teenager. Well, I *was* only seventeen when I made it.

As I swoop over the silent, still surface, I reach out a hand. My gloved fingertips cut through the water, sending up a bit of spray. It's cold. Really cold. Trying not to shiver, I pull up and away from the surface of the lake.

After flying to the far side, staying high enough that I won't be seen by any insomniacs who happen to glance out the window, I make a wide turn and fly back along the treed shoreline. My wings are starting to burn a little, but I know I've got enough gas in the tank to make it back to the park. (See? I may not be able to drive, but at least I know enough to make use of car metaphors.)

I make a sharp right at the willow, turning on my side. The backs of my wings brush against the leaves with a hissing *whisp*. Coming out of the curve, I flap hard, gaining altitude once more, hoping to get high into the air before I reach Tegan's place.

As I pass above the field, I glance down at the house. The lights are off, as they usually are at this time of night, and the windows are dark. But . . .

Circling back and letting myself sink on the air currents a little, I notice the movement in one of the upper windows. I blink, sure I must be seeing things. Maybe it's a raccoon. Or an owl. That must be it.

But it isn't. As I make a second pass, my eyes make sense of the movement, of Tegan's head and arms as she leans halfway out the window. She's waving like she's trying to direct air traffic.

Which, I guess, she is.

I land in a crouch on the little piece of roof outside her window in a flap of wings that sends her hair flying. The grin on her face is wide as she grips the windowsill.

"I *knew* you weren't a penguin."

I give a little chirp of happiness, then clap my gloved hand over my mouth. She giggles.

"Quiet. Dad's sleeping."

"Why aren't *you* sleeping?"

"I didn't want to miss this." She leans her elbows on the sill and cocks her head to one side. "How long have you been flying?"

"How long have you been watching?"

"A couple of days. I got up to pee one night, and when I came back to bed I saw something *huge* fly past."

"I was trying to be inconspicuous."

"Well, you failed. But it doesn't matter. You can *fly*, Sam. Do you know how unbelievably awesome that is?"

"It is pretty cool." I shrug my shoulders. She gives me a withering look.

"It's cool? It's more than that. It's amazing. It's unbelievable. If it were me, I'd be doing a happy dance in the field."

For a brief moment, I wonder if she saw my celebratory jig after my first successful flight. She's hard to read sometimes.

"I got you something," she says, glancing back into her darkened room. "I'm not sure if I should give it to you now or on your actual birthday, though."

My teeth click in surprise. "My birthday?"

"Yeah. Tomorrow. Or . . . well, I guess it's today, actually. Hold on." She moves away from the window, only to return a moment later. Something dark wriggles in her hands. As she holds it out toward me, I see the whiskers and the pink tail dangling from between her fingers. "Happy birthday, Sam."

I blink, but make no move to take the rat from her. "Where did you get it?"

"The pet store. He was pretty cheap, 'cause nobody wants black rats. They look too much like sewer rats, or so the guy at the store said. But I thought . . . they probably all taste the same, right?"

"Did you name him?"

She grimaces. "Yeah. Kind of."

"What?"

"Ludwig."

"Ludwig," I repeat, finally holding out my hand toward

the rat. When my gloved finger touches the top of his head, he wriggles hard. Tegan adjusts her grip. "Well," I say, trying to sound sad about it, "now that you've named him Ludwig, I don't think I can eat him."

"You ate Linda."

"I didn't like the name Linda."

"Omigod, Sam." She grins and pushes the rat toward me. I withdraw my hand and brace myself against the roof.

"Thank you. But I . . . I think I've developed an allergy."

"An allergy?"

"Yeah. If I eat him, I might swell up like a balloon. It's the fur, I think."

She gives me a suspicious look. I can tell she knows what I'm doing. "Uh-huh." She turns around, and I hear a rustle and a clink of metal as she returns Ludwig to his cage. When she returns, brushing the wood shavings from her fingers, I let out a sigh of relief.

"Thank you for thinking of me, though."

"You're welcome, Sam." She's gone back to leaning her elbows against the windowsill and staring at me. Her gaze is almost wistful. I pull my wings tight against my back.

"So . . . it's October thirty-first?" I ask.

"All day." She stares at me for a moment longer. Then her eyes visibly light up. She leans toward me, and I feel a sinking sensation in my gut. "Sam, can I ask you something?"

"I guess."

"Do you want to go to a party with me?"

I cough in disbelief, and my teeth click together of their own accord. "What?"

"A party. Tonight. Do you want to go with me?"

"Um . . ." I look down at my naked form, an almost indistinguishable shadow crouching on that little piece of roof. "I don't think that's a good idea."

She laughs with a shake of her head. "No, actually, it's a great idea. It's Halloween, Sam. It's a costume party." She stands up and leans out the window toward me. I'm kind of afraid she's going to tumble right out, so I edge sideways until I'll be able to block her fall if she does just that. "It's at Gabe's house. He lives down by the lake. All the grade twelves are invited. There'll be lots of people there, and everybody's going to be dressed up."

"I don't think I can blend in, even at a costume party."

"Well, no. Not like that." She waves a hand toward me, indicating my naked body. "But I've got a great idea for your costume. For both of our costumes. Please say you'll come, Sam. Please?"

I can't deny that the idea is appealing. I haven't been to a party with people my own age in over a decade . . . and I'm sure the sort of party Tegan's talking about now isn't the sort to feature a bouncy castle and blue birthday cake, like the last one I went to. The idea of mingling with a bunch of people in an enclosed space makes my whole body clench with anxiety. But it *is* a costume party . . . so it just might work.

"Please, Sam? I'll get everything set up. I'll bring a costume for you, and we can meet somewhere before the party so you can get dressed. All you have to do is say yes."

I click my teeth and stare out into the night. There are

fewer than twenty-four hours until the curse is finalized. And this might be my only chance to do one normal teenage thing before that happens. I turn back to Tegan.

"Do I have to wear pants?"

"Omigod, Sam." She dissolves into a fit of giggles. "What do you think?"

• 27 •

Sam Woroniecki, Intermunicipal Man of Mystery

After we agree to meet at seven o'clock that evening in the vacant lot just past the willow tree, Tegan straps a watch to my wrist and sends me off with half a carton of eggs. I wait until I get back home until I start to eat, forcing myself to finish all of them even though my stomach is turning itself inside out in nervous knots.

Did I really just agree to go to a party with a girl? I'm pretty sure this isn't a date, but that doesn't make me any less anxious about the whole thing. What if somebody figures out I'm not just a regular teenage guy in a costume? I don't want Tegan to get into any trouble, and I'm sure there would be trouble of some kind if people found out she brought a monster to the party. She told me to trust her . . . but I'm not sure I do. She's looking at all of this through her own lens of acceptance. Just because she's never been afraid of me or thought I was something to be shunned (or run out of town at the points of a pitchfork) doesn't mean everyone else is going to feel the same way.

I stay close to my nest all day, tidying and re-tidying it (even though it's already pretty tidy since I had to remake it after the black bird's demise). I glance at the watch every five minutes, clicking my teeth in annoyance whenever I see how little the hands have moved.

At five o'clock, as the light begins to dim, I take a bath in the stream, washing everywhere I can reach, careful not to dunk the watch in the water. I dry off by flapping my wings hard, but that sends a cloud of leaf debris swirling, and it sticks to my wet skin. Then I have to bathe all over again.

At last, it's ten minutes to seven. I run through the trees, burst onto the field, spread my shaking wings, and take to the air. When I arrive at the appointed spot, I'm a couple of minutes early, but Tegan is already there, waiting, perched on the driver's seat of her father's old pickup truck, her legs dangling out the open door.

"That's a costume?" I ask, looking her up and down. She's dressed in dark colours, with a leather jacket, boots, and a pair of jeans that might be brown . . . or just filthy.

"Well, it's not the *whole* costume," she says. "I can't be a demon hunter without weapons, can I?" She gestures to the two belts of fake-looking knives lying on the passenger seat. "I can't exactly drive with those on, though. Too awkward. And it would be *really* awkward if I got pulled over."

It's going to be really awkward if she gets pulled over with *me* in the truck, but I don't say that. She jumps to the ground and walks around to the back, then pulls out a bulging garbage bag and plunks it on the ground in front of her.

"The light's not great here, so we'll do any final adjustments at Krissy's if we need to."

"Krissy's?" My voice comes out in a squeak. "You didn't say anything about Krissy."

"Didn't I? Well, we're going over there after we get you dressed, and she's going to help me with my hair and makeup. Then we'll all drive over to the party."

"You're joking."

"No, Sam. I'm not." She rummages in the bag and pulls out some dark-coloured clothing. I can see something sparkle in the faint light. "Now, put these on. You ... um ... you do know how to put on pants, don't you?"

I click my teeth at her as I snatch the black jeans. My toe claws catch on the fabric when I push my feet through the legs, but I manage to get them on.

"I cut through the seam at the back for your tail," she says, just as I'm trying to hitch the jeans up around my waist. It's with more than a little relief that I work my tail through the hole. "How are they?"

I reach down the front and adjust some stuff. "Fine."

"Okay. Just . . . don't do *that* when we get there." She holds out the next piece, which appears to be a long black coat. Fancy braid sparkles on the cuffs, and fake brass buttons adorn the front. "This was part of a pirate costume at one point, I think. Nobody but you is going to be able to wear it now, though." She helps me get my arms into the sleeves, then pulls the whole thing over my head. She's cleverly sliced the back of the coat with two long slits to accommodate my wings, leaving a long flap that covers my hump and stretches all the way down to my tail. I adjust the garment, trying to make it sit properly on my shoulders.

"It's too big," I say, holding up my hands. The cuffs almost cover them. She shakes her head.

"It's regal. You're supposed to be a demon king, remember? Your clothes aren't supposed to be practical." She shoves the long black boots at me. I lean against the side of the truck to pull them on. They're also a bit too big, but at least I'm not going to get ingrown toe claws from them. When I'm clad to my knees in imitation leather, I step away from the truck and hold out my arms.

"How do I look?"

"Oh, we're not done yet."

"We're not?"

"No, we're not. We can pass your wings and tail off as part of your costume, and your teeth as a mask, but if anyone looks too closely at your ears and nose, there's going to be a problem."

"I don't have ears or a nose."

"Exactly." She pulls something black and sparkly from the bag and holds it up in front of me. I click my teeth at the sight of the sequinned mask.

"I don't have ears or a nose. How is that going to stay on?"

"Oh, ye of little faith." She pulls a roll of double-sided tape from the bag and arches an eyebrow at me. I sigh heavily in resignation. "Well, how else do you suggest keeping it on?" she asks as she applies short strips of tape to the mask all around the eye holes. After pulling off the backing, she reaches out toward me. "Hold still. I don't want to get this crooked."

"Yeah . . . a crooked mask is what everybody will be looking at."

"Shut up and hold still, Sam." She presses the mask against my face and steps back. "Huh."

"What?"

"You just look a little . . ."

"Stupid?"

"Yes, Sam. You look stupid." She rolls her eyes and reaches for the bag again. Her hand pulls out what looks like a small, black animal. She proceeds to place it on my head. "Now you look even more stupid. But at least nobody can see your ears."

"Lack of ears."

"You know, I'm starting to regret that I asked you to come."

"So am I."

She gives me a playful shove. I stagger back a couple of steps in my unfamiliar-feeling boots, but she grabs my arm before I can go too far. The last item in the bag looks sort of like one of the rings from an old stovetop burner, but it's been painted gold, and there are some plastic jewels glued around the circumference.

"What is that?" I ask as she places it on top of the wig, settling it down so it rests on my forehead.

"It's your crown, Your Highness." She takes a step back, adjusts the "crown" once more, and folds her arms across her chest in satisfaction. "You look awesome."

"I'll have to take your word for it."

She shakes her head. "You can see for yourself when we get to Krissy's."

Crap. I almost forgot. "Have you told her about me?"

She picks up the empty bag, ties it in a knot, and tosses it into the back of the truck before climbing up into the driver's seat. "Well, I told her I was bringing a friend. I didn't tell her anything about you, though. I mean, not what you are."

"What *did* you tell her?"

"Just that you're a friend I met online, and you just moved to the area and you don't know anyone, so I thought you might like to come to the party." She slams the door, then gestures for me to go around and get into the passenger seat. I stay put for so long that she rolls down the window. "Are you coming?"

"I don't think I'll fit." I spread my wings a little to demonstrate. She chews on her lip.

"I forgot about that."

"You forgot I had wings?"

"Just get in the back, smartass. Krissy's house is only a few blocks from here."

She starts the truck with a rumbling cough before I can protest again, so I have no choice but to climb up into the bed of the truck. I lie down on my stomach, feeling the brassy buttons dig into my chest as the truck lurches under Tegan's heavy-footed application of the gas pedal.

I'm feeling a little nauseated by the time the truck stops. I hop out on shaky legs and lean against the side with a heavy sigh.

"She doesn't bite, Sam."

"But I do."

"She doesn't know that. As far as she's concerned, you're just a college guy with a really amazing makeup job."

"You told her I was in college?"

She shrugs. "You're smart enough to be. You know more about calculus than I do, anyway." Tilting her head toward the front door of a house that looks like Halloween threw up on it, she gives me an encouraging smile.

"Your father would kill me if he knew we were doing this," I say.

"He'd want to kill you no matter what. Don't worry about him, Sam."

"Is he okay with you going to this party?"

She rolls her eyes. "He practically begged me to go. He still thinks I got seduced by some demonic chupacabra in the woods, so any time I act like a regular teenager, it makes him really happy."

"I'm not a chupacabra." My voice comes out sounding almost whiny.

"Don't sulk. It's unbecoming of a demon king." When I sigh again, she takes my gloved hand and leads me up to the front door.

Before Krissy can even get the door open, Tegan lets out an exaggerated "Trick-or-treat!" followed by a laugh. Krissy laughs right back at her, and, with nothing but a quick, curious glance in my direction, stands aside so we can enter.

"So . . . you're Sam?" she says as she starts to lead us up the stairs.

I nod, and then, realizing she's turned away and can't see me, add a quick, "Yes."

"His makeup makes it hard to understand him," Tegan puts in quickly. Krissy shakes her head a little, as if in disbelief.

"Yeah, but it's worth it. It's amazing."

I glance at Tegan through the mask and feel her give my hand a squeeze.

In Krissy's bedroom, I hover by the doorway as the girls finish putting the finishing touches on their costumes. Krissy is dressed as some sort of pre-Revolution French princess, complete with white wig and ridiculously ruffly dress. She applies rouge to her cheeks and a beauty mark to her upper lip, then helps Tegan braid her dark hair in some elaborate way that I'm sure has a name I'm not familiar with.

"So," Krissy says as she reaches for a makeup pencil and proceeds to sketch a hideous-looking wound across Tegan's perfect skin. "You're the demon that gave her this."

"Oh, he did much worse than that," Tegan says, casting a wicked glance in my direction. Krissy laughs.

"Yeah. I'm sure. I can't believe you threw this costume together at the last minute."

"Well, when I heard about Sam's costume, I wanted something that would go with it. I didn't think my old fairy costume from last year would've stood up against *that*." She waves one hand in my direction. "I mean, my wings were made from wire and a pair of tights."

I resist the urge to wiggle my wings. They're supposed to be fakes. Very real-looking fakes.

"The thrift store had everything I needed," Tegan goes on. "I barely had to spend anything." The wound now stretches from the inside corner of her right eye, across her nose, and down her left cheek. It totally looks like something my claws might do if I weren't careful.

"I bet your costume cost a fortune."

I don't realize Krissy's talking to me until she turns around, makeup pencil still in hand. I look at Tegan in desperation, and finally just decide on a shrug. Krissy smirks.

"So you're the strong, *silent* type, eh?" She turns back to Tegan and reaches for another facial-writing implement to make a series of fine stitches along the horrible-looking wound. "Well, they do say opposites attract."

"Hey! I'm not that loud."

"Seriously, Tee? You're not quiet, either." She caps the pen and tosses it on the dresser. "How's that?"

Tegan turns to the mirror and examines her new wound. "Looks good." She turns around and reaches her hand toward me. "Come here, Sam."

Hesitantly, I put one foot in front of the other and somehow manage to cross the room. Krissy watches me the whole time, and I feel like she can see right through the coat and mask. I keep my gaze on Tegan as I approach. When I'm close enough, she snags my hand and pulls me toward her so I'm standing at her side.

"It'll be better once I get my weapons on, but you get the idea." Her gaze meets mine through the mirror. "Pretty cool, right?"

It is. She looks fierce and beautiful, like she could slay an entire army of my kind with just a look. As for me . . . well, I look regal, like she said earlier. And, with the mask and the wig, it does sort of look like I'm simply dressed up in an elaborate costume. I try to stand a little straighter as I manage to choke out, "Yeah. It is."

"Party starts at eight," Krissy says, fumbling in the bottom of her closet for a pair of shoes. She holds a grey-and-chartreuse runner up in one hand. "Do you think anyone will notice if I wear these? The dress is pretty long . . ."

"Why would you want to wear those?" Tegan asks.

"They're comfortable. Besides . . . you never know when you might need to do some running."

Tegan laughs. "I don't know what kind of party you're expecting."

"It's best to be prepared, isn't it?" The princess shucks her socks and pulls the shoes onto her bare feet before heading for the bedroom door. I shrink back as she brushes past me, and Tegan gives my arm a reassuring squeeze. "You're driving, right?" Krissy asks. "I don't think I can in this dress." She holds her hands over the wide panniers at her hips.

"Yeah. Dad's truck is outside."

As we walk back to the front door, I feel something soft brush against my wing. My first instinct is to shrink away, but I remember I'm not supposed to be able to feel anything.

"Those wings are really, really cool," Krissy says behind me. "What are they made of? Silicone?"

"Something like that," I mumble.

Back outside in the cold night air, the girls make a rush for the heated cab of the truck. There's no room for me in there now, especially with Krissy's dress, so I climb up into the bed of the truck and lie down like I did before.

The drive to this Gabe person's house is smoother than the one to Krissy's, but that's probably because there aren't as many turns. When Tegan parks the truck along the shoulder of the road, gravel crunching under the tires, I can already hear the sounds of a party underway. Leaping lightly from the back, I land next to the driver's door. Tegan stows her keys in her pocket and reaches for her belts of weapons. She buckles one around her hips and slings the other over her shoulders, careful not to disturb her freshly braided hair.

"Don't kill me," I say with an exaggerated nervous glance at the row of fake knives across her chest. She gives me an appraising look, one eyebrow cocked high.

"I'm a demon hunter. It's what I do. So you'd better watch out, Your Highness." She slams the truck's door closed, then opens it again to talk to Krissy, who's still huddled in the front seat. "You coming?"

"It's freezing out there. I should've brought my jacket."

"Marie Antoinette didn't wear a puffer jacket."

Krissy grumbles something unintelligible as she pulls herself out of the far side of the truck. I take the opportunity to step closer to Tegan. She looks up.

"Stay with me," I say. "I . . . I've never been to a party like this."

She lets out a small laugh and reaches up to straighten my crown. "You'll be fine. Nobody has any reason to suspect a thing. Most of them don't even believe in things like you, so they have no reason to suspect anything." She pauses, wincing. "I mean . . . not that you're a *thing*, Sam. I meant—"

"I know."

"Okay." She brightens her expression as Krissy stumbles around the back of the truck, picking at her skirt.

"Try to park outside the bushes next time, Tee." She gives us a quick once-over and shakes her head as she walks past. "I wish *I* had a boyfriend I could do the whole costume thing with."

"I'm not—" I begin, but Tegan pokes me in my bare chest and gives me a warning glance.

"For tonight, you are," she whispers. "Try not to look too disappointed about it." Then she takes my hand and follows Krissy down the long driveway toward the sounds of the party.

• 28 •

Party Animal

It hits us in a blast of music, raised voices, the scent of pizza, and air warmed by what looks like about a hundred kids. I pull my wings against my back so tightly that it feels like I might pull a muscle.

Everybody's in costume, and though I get a few curious and appreciative glances as we walk into the large foyer, I don't seem to draw an unusual amount of attention.

"There's Gabe," Tegan says, her voice loud next to my ear. She points across the space and waves to a tall blond kid who's dressed up as a Roman emperor. When he sees us, he flashes a white-toothed grin and hurries over, his burgundy cape rippling behind him. On Tegan's other side, Krissy makes an audible yelp that sounds almost like one of my chirps. When I glance at her, the rest of her face has caught up to her rouged cheeks.

"Hey," Gabe says, sauntering to a stop in front of us. He

looks like he should be leading an annoying boy band or starring in a movie on one of those TV channels for tween girls. His gaze sweeps over Tegan, then moves on to me. One side of his mouth curls up in a smirk, revealing a deep dimple in his cheek. "Awesome costume," he says, nodding his head toward me. "Is that makeup?" His gaze is on my bare chest. I nod quickly. He shakes his head in disbelief. "That's one hell of a commitment to Halloween."

"Oh, he takes all of this *very* seriously," Tegan says, giving me a nudge in the ribs, as if she wants me to say something. What am I supposed to say? I panic for a moment, and clench my jaw to keep my teeth from clicking.

"Thanks for inviting us," I say at last. Gabe just shrugs.

"The more the merrier, right?" He pauses, his head tilted slightly to the side as if he's deep in thought. "So . . . who are you?"

"He's my friend," Tegan says quickly. "Sam. He graduated last year. I hope it was okay to bring him."

"Sure. We've got plenty of pizza. What's one more person?" He flashes Tegan a dazzling smile, and I feel her sort of melt against my side. I wonder what it would be like to have that effect on girls.

Or, you know, any effect other than pee-your-pants terror.

"Um . . . I guess we'll go check out the snacks," Tegan says, and begins to pull me farther into the house. Gabe watches us go—well, actually, he watches *her* go—before finally turning to greet the newcomers that have just come up behind us at the door.

Krissy's blush has spread down to her exposed cleavage.

She looks down at the tops of her pink breasts and shakes her head. "Kill me now."

Tegan grabs a handful of caramel corn and lets go of me to pop a piece into her mouth. "Why?"

Krissy shakes her head in disbelief, her eyes wide. "I just stood there like an idiot. He's so hot, I think he fried my brain."

"He's all right."

"Says the girl he couldn't peel his eyes off of. I'm practically hanging out of my dress, and he couldn't look away from the girl covered in leather up to her neck."

"It's not real leather."

"Yeah, Tee. That's kind of not the point." She grabs her own handful of caramel corn and proceeds to fumble one of the kernels into her cleavage. "Shit."

"You could go ask Gabe to fish that out for you. I'm sure he'd oblige."

"Shut up," Krissy says, but I can tell she's on the verge of laughter. She pops the rest of the kernels into her mouth, then grabs Tegan's elbow. "Come on. *You're* going to help me fish it out. It's already getting sticky. I can feel it."

Tegan shoots me an apologetic look as she lets Krissy haul her away. But what am I supposed to do? I'm eighteen, and I should be able to handle a party without a babysitter. I pretend to peruse the snack table. I don't see any bowls of raw eggs or platters of uncooked chicken wings, so I move on, trying to act casual as I drift through the space.

There are kids everywhere. A couple of risqué fairies are squeezed into one straining easy chair, taking selfies. An old-school vampire with plastic fangs sits on the table in the kitchen next to a girl dressed as a sexy cat. Well, she's sort of dressed. The skimpy skirt seems to be no match for the vampire, who has his hand up it. I look away and continue drifting slowly through the room.

Near the back of the house is another living area, this one somewhat casual. Through a set of glass doors, I can see the backyard lit up with strings of lights. Some of the party seems to have spilled out there; a few groups of kids are huddled in clumps on the lawn.

"Dude. That costume is amazing. Where'd you get it?"

I turn around, assuming (correctly) that someone is speaking to me. The kid is short, his dark hair messy. It actually looks like he rubbed dirt into it. I guess that's to go with the grime that's smeared all over his torn clothes. Fake blood has dried around his mouth and on his chin.

"I made it."

"Even the wings?" Another zombie appears beside the first. This one has darker skin, and the pale makeup he's applied makes him look kind of grey.

"Yeah."

"Awesome," the first kid says. "You look like . . . Sanjay, what's that thing called?"

"What thing?"

"You know. That winged beast in *Quest Summons*. In the Caves of Mucosia mission."

Sanjay gives him a blank look, but I know exactly what he's talking about.

"The gryhopper?"

"Yes!" The first kid snaps his fingers and points at me. I nod.

"That's what I based it on. But the gryhopper doesn't have a tail."

"It doesn't wear clothes, either," Sanjay says. "Wait. You have a tail?"

"Yeah."

The first kid laughs. "You really went all out. What are you supposed to be, anyway?"

"Demon king."

"Allen and I are zombies," Sanjay says.

"Thank you, Captain Obvious." Allen shakes his head. "So, you play *Quest Summons?*" he asks me.

"Yeah. I got to the Cerulean Pool last month. I've been kind of stuck there ever since."

"Shit," Sanjay mutters. "I never made it past the Treetop Massacre."

"That's 'cause you suck." Allen gets up without another word and strolls into the kitchen. I glance at Sanjay, somewhat confused. I may not be an expert on social interaction with teenagers, but I'm pretty sure that's not how you end a conversation. Allen returns a few seconds later, though, three cans of pop in his hands. He hands one to Sanjay and one to me, then pops the top of his and takes a slurping gulp. His bloody lips are a little less red now. I set the can down on the shelf of the bookcase beside me.

"Can't drink anything . . . with this mask."

"Oh," Allen says. "Sorry."

I shrug and pretend like it doesn't bother me. Sanjay cracks open his can and drains half of it in one go.

"You're not from around here," Allen guesses.

"Uh . . . no."

"I figured. Sanjay and I know all the gamers at school, and none of them have gotten to the Cerulean Pool." He taps his dirty fingernails against the can. "So . . ."

"I'm Sam. Tegan's friend."

Allen looks at Sanjay, his forehead creasing in confusion for a moment. "Oh. Tegan Morales."

"She's cute," Sanjay says quietly.

"She's obnoxious," Allen says, not so quietly. "But I guess you already know that, don't you?"

I shrug noncommittally. A few weeks ago, I might've said the same thing. Tegan hasn't really changed since then, but . . . I don't really mind so much now.

"Where'd you meet her, anyway?" Allen asks.

"Online."

"Gaming?"

I shake my head, but I'm not sure how, exactly, we were supposed to have met. Maybe she's secretly one of those girl gamers that kicks the crap out of the boys and then gets harassed because of it. Anything's possible.

"You should see the system Gabe's got here," Sanjay says. "I would *kill* to have a set-up like that."

"Yeah, well, it helps when your parents are loaded." Allen takes another slurpy sip. Bit by bit, the blood on his lips is disappearing. "He probably doesn't have to spend all his allowance if he wants new games."

"He probably gets more allowance than my dad makes in a week," Sanjay adds.

I'm not quite sure what to say to any of that. My games usually appeared like the rats. I never knew their origin, but they turned up in my room all the same. And I never really asked. There were quite a few of them, though, and they must've cost quite a bit.

"Are you hungry?" Allen asks.

"Yeah." Sanjay detaches himself from the wall and heads for the kitchen. When I shake my head at Allen's raised eyebrows, he shrugs and follows his friend. I let out a small breath of relief and pretend to be interested in the books on the shelf.

Actually, I don't have to pretend too hard. If I knew Gabe better, I might ask him if I could borrow one or two. There are books about medical history, rare medical conditions and syndromes, cutting-edge treatments and advances in genetic diseases. Definitely not the type of book I'd feel like shredding in frustration after reading. Gabe didn't particularly strike me as the studious type—although, I should know better than anyone that looks can be deceiving—but someone in this family has great taste in reading material.

My gaze skims over the titles on the shelf that's just about at eye level. The row of books is broken by a framed photo of two little kids, a boy and a girl. I can tell the little blond boy is Gabe; the deep dimple in one cheek gives him away. The older girl must be his sister. There's something . . . familiar about the two of them. I can't quite figure out what it is. Maybe they remind me of someone I used to know back before the transformation. Did I go to school with one of them at some point? I peer closer. The boy's round-cheeked face reminds me of something . . .

"Sam."

No. Not some*thing*. Some*one*. The instantly recognizable voice sends a chill up my spine, and my wings tremble before I can stop them. I turn slowly, my heart hammering in my chest, knowing what I'm going to see but unwilling to believe it.

Dr. Grant stares at me, his eyes cold. With a glance that rakes up and down my costumed body, his face puckers into a sour frown.

"We need to have a talk."

• 29 •

Aw, Crap

As Dr. Grant leads me to the stairs, I glance around desperately, searching for Tegan. I have no idea what's going to happen now, but I'm pretty sure it isn't going to be good.

Why did I ever agree to come to this stupid party?

I climb the stairs like I'm walking up to the gallows, and follow Dr. Grant down the hallway. At the end, he leads me into a small office and flicks on the light.

"Close the door."

I do as he says, slowly, as if I can stall and prevent this conversation from happening. But there's really not much you can do to drag out the closing of a door. As the latch clicks, I turn around. My gaze is stuck to the floor.

"Well?"

If he wants me to explain myself, he's going to be waiting a long time. My fists clench in my gloves.

"Sam. Look at me."

I slowly look up into Dr. Grant's eyes. They're expressionless, and that scares me more than anything.

"Do you have any idea the trouble you've caused?"

I nod slowly. He seems taken aback.

"Really. Tell me, Sam. Tell me all about what you've put me through. What you've put the staff through. What you've put your father through."

"My father?"

He sits down in the swivel chair behind the desk, a careful and overly precise movement that makes me think he's not entirely confident he's in control of his own body.

He's totally pissed off.

"Yes, Sam. Your father. Did you stop to think what you disappearing would do to him? I had to let him know. I thought you might try to contact him."

"Why would I do that?" A deep growl builds in my throat. "He left me there. With *you.*"

"It was the best place for you. It still is." He shakes his head slowly, as if he's just understood something. "Sam, he didn't want to leave you there. But he didn't know how to handle you. And, judging by some of the comments he made, I think he blames himself for what happened."

"Why?"

"Parents of children with genetic diseases often blame themselves."

Is that what Dad believes? That I have a disease? I slowly fold my arms over my chest and back up against the door, staying silent.

"Why did you run away, Sam?"

"Why do you think?"

"We've discussed this. Many times. And I know you want to experience a normal life, but that's not possible for you. You'll just have to accept that."

"I *am* experiencing a normal life. I'm here, aren't I? Nobody thinks I'm anything other than a kid in a costume."

"Tonight. But what about tomorrow, when everybody else takes off their costumes? What then?"

"That's not your problem."

Dr. Grant's brow furrows, and I know he hasn't caught that last word. Doesn't he know a "krodlen" when he sees one? I drop my arms to my sides and take a step toward him.

"Problem. It's not your *problem*. All I want is one night where I can be myself. Where I don't have to sit alone in a basement and eat rats."

"You're not completely cut off from the outside world. I let you have an internet connection."

"It's not the same!" I roar. Dr. Grant's eyes flash dangerously.

"Keep your voice down." He stands up and pulls a set of keys from his pocket. After unlocking a cabinet on the wall, he pulls a flat box from the shelf within. "Sam, when your father left you in my care, you became my responsibility. I take that duty very seriously."

"No kidding."

He ignores me and continues. "I know you're lonely. But you don't belong here. If anyone found out what you are . . . well, you know what would happen."

I snort. The resulting squeak sounds loud in the small office.

"I'm not happy about you being here," he goes on, ignoring my little outburst. "Not at all. After your escape from the hospital, I have my doubts as to whether I'll ever be able to trust you again."

I try to look contrite as I fix my gaze on the floor. My mind is whirling. I'm worrying about what's going to happen now, of course. But I'm also wondering how Dr. Grant thinks I ended up in his house, especially if he's assuming nobody's discovered my secret yet. Maybe he thinks I stalked him online or something.

"I'm not an unfair man, Sam. I know you don't see it that way right now, but one day, you will. One day, you'll thank me for protecting you from those who would try to hurt you. Those who would take you apart to see what makes you tick. So I'm going to make a deal with you."

"What kind of a deal?"

"You can stay for the party. Get it out of your system. And then, when it's over, you'll come back to the hospital with me, and we'll put tonight behind us."

"Like hell," I mutter. His eyes flash behind his glasses as he turns to the box and opens the lid. When I see what's inside, my heart drops into my stomach.

"If you don't behave yourself, Sam, I will use this." He loads the pistol with two tranquilizer darts and slides it into his waistband. I look up into his face in disbelief as he walks toward me, takes my arm, and steers me to the door. "Now, go enjoy yourself. But know that I'm keeping an eye on you. And if I see you do anything remotely stupid, if I think that any of these kids are in danger, I won't hesitate to use this."

"And how would you explain shooting one of your son's party guests?"

"Let's not find out." He reaches past me to open the door,

then lets go of my arm as he shoves me ahead of him. I stumble on the hall runner as I look back. The flap of his open cardigan hides the gun, but there's no mistaking the dangerous look in his eyes.

I make my way back down the stairs, resisting the urge to kick out all the spindles in the banister. But I know that would get me shot before I could remodel even half the staircase.

I have to get out of here. Dr. Grant might be watching, but what's he going to do? I can fly. He can't. If I can get out of this house, and out of this costume, then I have a chance at making an escape.

And then what? Everybody knows I came with Tegan, and if Dr. Grant finds that out, he'll start watching her, too. I won't be able to see her anymore. Not without risking getting caught and dragged back to the hospital, probably in a net.

Like the animal Dr. Grant thinks I am.

I guess what happened during my escape didn't help with that impression, but what's done is done. I don't know how to convince him otherwise. Even walking around in jeans, a coat, and boots doesn't seem to make him think of me as anything close to human.

I find Krissy near the snack table, an anachronistic tableau of Marie Antoinette eating a greasy slice of pizza. She looks up, startled, when I touch her shoulder.

"Where's Tegan?"

"No idea." She licks a blob of tomato sauce from her lip and gives me a shrug. "She was talking to Gabe a while ago."

"Did she go somewhere with him?"

"I don't know, Sam." She sounds annoyed. I back up a

step and survey the room. A few kids are dancing, and homemade costumes are losing bits and pieces to the movement. There's a roar of laughter as a kid dressed as a house loses his cardboard front porch.

It's too hot in here. I need some air. Dr. Grant might think I'm trying to escape, but I don't care. If I don't get out of this house now, I don't know what I might do.

I stagger onto the back patio and press my hands against my knees as I take in a few gulps of cool air. Someone closes the door behind me, muffling the music. It's not completely silent out here, though; I can hear murmured conversations, the rustle of clothes, even the smack of lips. After casting a quick glance at the couple making out right beside me, I straighten up and head out onto the lawn.

My boots slide against the dewy grass as I walk down the gentle slope. Directly in front of me, there's nothing to see except darkness. But, if I squint a little, I can just make out a horizontal band of lights sparkling faintly in the distance. I leave the party behind as I walk toward the water. It would be so easy to just spread my wings and fly away. But I've messed up, and now Tegan's involved. Even if I never try to see her again, Dr. Grant will probably be on her case, trying to find out what she knows, hoping to find out where I've gone . . . even if she has no idea. I blow out a frustrated breath through my nostrils, but since it's blocked by the mask, it doesn't make much noise at all.

A small figure suddenly storms out of the darkness from the direction of the lake. I freeze, my teeth clicking once in surprise before I can stop them. Tegan looks up and sees me standing there. Her cheeks are flushed, and she looks as angry as she did when she called me an ass after I dove out of the tree. Maybe even angrier. She reaches out to take my hand as she passes, trying to pull me back toward the house.

"I'm done," she says, her voice tight. "Let's go home."

"Why? What happened?"

She chews on her lip, then looks back toward the lake. I follow her gaze and see Gabe emerge from the shadows. He doesn't look very happy, either.

"Sam," Tegan says, tugging on my hand, "come on."

"Yeah, Sam." Gabe's voice is snide. He folds his muscled arms across his chest and plants his sandals as he comes to a stop in front of us. "Let her lead you on. Let's see how many guys the little whore can kiss in one evening."

I have to keep my mouth from dropping open. It's an effort. "What did you say?"

"I didn't lead you on," Tegan says, stepping forward but still clinging to my hand as if it gives her some sort of strength. "Apparently, I was confused. How was I supposed to know that 'Do you want to see my dad's boat?' meant the same thing as 'Do you want me to stick my tongue down your throat?'"

My head swivels toward Gabe, and I stare. He looks a little uncomfortable now. He looks even more uncomfortable when my low growl curls into the air.

"Whatever," he says, dropping his arms and walking past us, back toward the house. "Enjoy her while you can. Before she moves on to the next one."

"Sam. Sam, stop!" Tegan whispers desperately as I pull my hand from her grasp. Gabe turns back to me, his handsome face quirked in an arrogant smile.

"What? You're going to defend her *honour?*" He laughs. "You're probably a few screws too late for that."

I reach up and grab the shoulders of the coat, tearing it off. The wig and crown fall off as I do so. My gloved hands fumble awkwardly for the mask, and when I finally get a good grip, I pull it away and let it fall to the ground. Gabe's sneer is only enhanced by the creep of one perfect eyebrow toward his hairline.

"Is your makeup supposed to scare me?" He turns away with a shake of his head. "Freak."

The shriek that bursts out of me makes him stop in his tracks. He turns around slowly, just in time to see me raise my wings.

"What the hell?" he says, his voice a little more awed now, a little less cocky. "What kind of shit is this?"

"Sam! That's enough."

I look up, back toward the house, and see Dr. Grant running at us. I should've known this wasn't going to end well. Still, there are other kids outside, all now focused on the altercation between me and Gabe. I take a step back and look over at Tegan. Her eyes are wide as she stares at me, both hands plastered across her mouth.

So much for our charade.

"Go back in the house," Dr. Grant says, turning around to address the curious clusters of kids on the lawn. "Now!" When they start to go, wide-eyed and silent, he turns back toward us and storms across the grass.

"I didn't do anything," I say.

"We're going. Now." He jerks his thumb over his shoulder. "I'm taking you back right now."

"Taking him where?" Gabe asks. "Who is this guy?"

"He's one of my patients at the hospital. And he did *not* have permission to leave. Not in his condition."

I'm pretty sure letting that bit of information slip violates doctor-patient confidentiality, but I think Dr. Grant has gone well past the boundaries of medical ethics at this point.

"Why's he in the hospital?" Gabe asks, taking a step back. "Is he contagious?"

"No. He has a genetic condition. It affects . . . his digestive system. It causes psychiatric symptoms as well. Lack of judgment. Impulse-control problems."

My breath quickens as I tear off my gloves and hurl them into the darkness. Tegan lets out an audible gasp. Impulse-control problems? You bet I have impulse-control problems. I take a step toward Gabe, one clawed hand raised menacingly. My gaze is fixed on Dr. Grant the whole time, challenging him. It doesn't take much. He pulls the gun from his waistband and points it at me.

There's a burst of surprised exclamations from our audience, who are all huddled on the other side of the glass doors. Cutting above the other voices, I can clearly hear someone say, "Holy shit! He just pulled a gun on him." Someone else says, "This is awesome!"

They think it's a show. I'm about to lose my freedom, my life . . . and these kids think it's all for their entertainment. What do they know? How could they possibly understand what it's like to be me?

They can't.

Dr. Grant is right. I don't belong here. I'm not a normal teenager, no matter how much I'd like to be one. A normal teenager doesn't end the night staring into the barrel of a tranquilizer gun. I drop my hand.

"Tegan," I say. I look back at her, to where she's standing just a few feet away. Her face is crumpled, but whether it's in confusion or sadness, I can't tell. She must have so many questions. There's so much she doesn't understand. I'll probably never get a chance to tell her now. "I have to go."

"Go where?"

"With him. With Dr. Grant." I shake my head. "I'm sorry."

She stares at me in wide-eyed disbelief. I have to look away. "But why?" she asks.

"I'm sorry," I say again. Turning to Dr. Grant, I swallow all of the hateful words I long to sling at him. "All right. Let's go."

"No. Sam. Don't . . ."

I hear her before I see her, and the next thing I know, she's pressed against me, her head right next to mine, her arms thrown tightly around my neck. My teeth click in surprise. I hold my hands out awkwardly to the sides, terrified of nicking her with my claws.

"Don't go."

"I have to."

"No." Her face presses against my neck, and her breath is warm against my skin. I look up at Dr. Grant and give a helpless little shrug. He sighs and slowly lowers the gun.

"Tegan, I have to go."

She clings tighter, and I swear I can feel her heartbeat hammering against my chest. I just want this to be over with. I need her to let go. But she won't. And I can't risk trying to remove her arms myself.

"Sam," she whispers, her breath hot against my earhole. "Fly away. Fly away from here."

I blink and say nothing as I wait for her to let go of me. Still, she doesn't. This has got to be one of the longest good-bye hugs ever, and Gabe is starting to look a little disgusted. He turns away and starts to walk back to the house. Tegan tightens her arms even more.

All at once I understand what she wants me to do, and I know it's stupid and reckless and probably impossible, but at that moment it's either that or let Dr. Grant drive me back to the hospital so I can spend the rest of my days eating rats in the basement. I stretch out my wings, and Tegan pulls herself tight against my body, as if in confirmation. Keeping my hands tightly fisted and held out to the sides, I lower into a crouch. And then, before I can allow myself to imagine what will happen if this doesn't work, I jump into the air.

My wings strain as they flap hard, attempting to bear the weight of two bodies. When my feet don't come back onto the ground, when I hear a collective gasp from inside the house, when I see Dr. Grant's eyes widen in surprise and horror and disappointment, I know it's working.

"Holy shit!" Gabe screams as he scrambles backward, nearly tripping over his cape. I swoop up over the roof and land next to the chimney. Below us, though I can't see anything, the party has broken into pandemonium. I hear doors open and voices spill out into the night as partygoers rush to search the sky.

"You're crazy," I mutter to Tegan, who hasn't yet released her grip. "Where are we supposed to go now? They're going to follow us. And if Dr. Grant hits me with one of those darts, we'll crash."

"So? You heal fast."

"You don't."

She pulls back a little so she can look at my face. Being just inches away from my terrible teeth doesn't seem to faze her one bit. "You can't go with him."

"Tegan, I have nowhere else to go."

She turns and stares into the darkness. The breeze catches a few of the hairs that have come loose from her elaborate braid and blows them against the fake wound on her cheek. "Go across the lake."

"What?"

"You can make it, can't you?"

"Yes, but—"

"They won't be able to follow you. By the time they drive themselves to the other side, you'll be gone. Or hidden. We can figure that out when we get there."

"You're not coming with me."

She gives me a withering look. "So . . . what? You're going to leave me up here on the roof?"

Crap. She's got a point.

"Let's get going," she says. "The sooner we get away from that crazy doctor with the gun, the sooner we can figure all this out." She wraps her arms around my neck once more. I think about protesting, but I know this is one argument I'm not going to win.

"Hold on tight."

In response, she sort of jumps up and wraps her legs around my hips. I take a deep breath and charge to the edge of the roof. There's a horrible moment when I think I've miscalculated, when we start to plummet to the ground. But then my open wings catch the air. My boots nearly graze the top of Dr. Grant's balding head as we swoop over him where he stands in the grass, searching the sky. He ducks, almost too late, with a shout.

"Damn it, Sam! Come back here!"

Does he really think I will? I flap hard, and the ground disappears beneath us, replaced with the shadowy surface of the lake. It's too dark to see our reflections in the smooth water. I keep my head up, my gaze fixed on the distant lights.

A sharp prick, followed by a horrible stinging sensation in my left wing, causes me to shriek in terror as we tilt precariously close to the water, but I manage to recover my stride quickly. It takes a moment before I realize what's happened.

Within seconds, my wing starts to feel numb. I don't know exactly how much time I've got before the tranquilizer takes me down, but I know it isn't long. What do I do? Turn around and head back to land? We're already kind of far out over the water. I don't know if I'd make it. Even if I did, we'd be in for a rough landing, and Tegan would be hurt.

Maybe worse.

I blink hard, forcing my eyes to stay open, and work to keep my wings pumping in a synchronized rhythm. We're a little more than halfway across now. Luckily, the lake is oblong and we're flying across one of the narrowest parts. But it's still quite a distance. And I know I'm not going to make it.

"Do you know how to swim?" I ask. When she doesn't answer, I raise my voice and call a little louder.

"Yes," comes the answer.

"Then you need to—" My head drops forward onto her shoulder. Just like that. I pull it back up and click my teeth, as if I can intimidate myself into staying awake. "You need to let go."

"No way."

"I'm not going . . . to make it." I can barely fly and talk at the same time anymore. We dip low as I speak, my wings awkward in their rhythm, and the toes of my boots scrape the surface of the water. I pump my wings as hard as I can, trying to regain the lost altitude. The lights are coming closer; we're still over the lake, but if Tegan can swim, she can make it to the shore. "You need to . . . let go."

She tightens her arms around my neck. Her legs squeeze my hips. I let out a gasp of desperation.

"Let go. Please . . . let go." If she doesn't, if we go down like this, she'll be forced under by the weight of my body.

I can barely keep my eyes open now. My voice comes in rasping cries.

"Let go. Please . . . Please!" I feel the muscles in my arms and legs go limp. Everything feels warm. My head falls forward. "Please, Tegan . . ."

My toes drag along the surface for the final clumsy wingbeats. And then I can't move. I feel my limp wings crumple onto the surface of the water as we slam into it. The cold is like fire, seeping into my mouth and hitting my tongue like a million needles. Tegan's body is under mine, still clinging as she's pushed under by the weight of me. She won't let go. Why won't she let go?

She's going to die. No. This can't be happening. This can't . . .

No. I'm sorry.

I . . .

Tegan . . .

No . . .

• 30 •

Not a Penguin After All

White mist swirls above me when I open my eyes. It's brighter than in the dream. And colder. I close my eyes and shiver violently.

A heavy weight presses on my right shoulder, against my side. I take a deep breath and open my eyes again, turning my head so I can see what it is. Dark brown hair. The top of someone's head. Tegan. She's not moving.

I killed her. Oh, my god. I killed her. My breath quickens, and I see her head rise and fall as it rides on my chest.

She's still warm.

But . . . that can't be right. It's obviously been hours since we flew over—no, fell into—the lake. Her body would've cooled by now, especially after being in that cold water.

Suddenly, she stirs, and I feel the warmth of her sigh as it spreads across my bare chest. I close my eyes again in relief. My body seems to lurch under me, and I feel like I'm spinning sideways.

Tranquilizers. Such lovely instruments of torture.

Off to my left, I can hear the gentle lapping of water. Against the backs of my hands, grainy sand scratches at my skin. How did this happen? How are we both still alive? I open my eyes once more.

There's something on my face, between my eyes. I can't really feel it, but I can see it. I reach up to remove whatever it is . . . and freeze.

"Oh, my god."

Tegan stirs, and I feel her fingers press against my chest. She raises her head slowly, blinking. As she takes in my face and my shaking hand hovering just above it, her eyes go wide.

"What is this?" My breath comes in quick gasps. I stare at her, as if she can give me an answer. As if she can explain what I'm seeing. I turn my hand over in disbelief, watching a fine charcoal dust slide from my pasty skin. The same substance is plastered to the side of her face, nearly obliterating the remains of her fake wound. "What is this?"

She pulls back as I haul myself into a sitting position. The grainy dust slides from my arms and chest, falling onto the dew-damp sand. I hold my hands in front of me. My fingers look so short now. The tips are smooth and rounded. There are no fingernails at all, but there are no claws, either. Shaking violently, I raise those fingers to my face. They find a nose. Cheeks. A chin with a divot, like the one I remember from so many years ago, only more pronounced. And lips. I have lips! I part them with one finger and run the fingertip over the teeth within. They're slightly crooked, but blunt.

When I pull my finger back out and stare at it, there's no cut. There's no blood.

"What happened?" I whisper. "What happened?"

But what answer is there? For the first time in eleven years, I begin to cry. I feel the tears pour out of me, streaking down my cheeks. I cover my face with my hands and bend forward over my legs, sobbing.

I almost forget she's there with me until she gently takes my wrists and pulls my hands from my face. I turn my head away, not wanting her to see this blubbering mess.

"Sam?"

"Yeah." I shake my head and try to wipe the tears away with the back of one hand. "Not what you expected, is it?"

"You're not kidding." Her eyes are wide. "What the heck is going on? What are you?"

I laugh. It still sounds disused and rusty, but not so unnatural.

"I'm free," I tell her.

"You're three?"

"Fffree," I say, testing my front teeth against my bottom lip. Great. I'm going to need speech therapy.

"Free from what?" she asks, then shakes her head. "Never mind. I don't care." And she takes my face in her hands and kisses me.

I blink in surprise. I'm not sure what to do. I'm not sure I could make my lips do what I wanted them to at this point, anyway. But Tegan doesn't seem to mind. She pulls back with a smile, then wraps her arms around my neck. I feel her hands, chilled by the morning air, rub over my shoulders.

"Your wings are gone."

"Gone?"

She pulls away and nods, gesturing to the area behind me. I turn to look, and more grey dust falls from my shoulders. It's smeared across my skin, darkening it like I've been crawling around in soot. The same dust lies in a vaguely wing-shaped pattern on the sand. I get up onto my hands and knees and stare at it.

"Holy crap."

"I always knew you weren't a penguin." She gestures at the shadowy outlines. "Looks like you were more of a phoenix."

"Rising from the ashes . . ." I say quietly, still staring at the remains of the curse.

"No more flying now." Her voice sounds sad. I turn to her in disbelief. "Aren't you going to miss it?"

Well, maybe a little. "Not the crash landings," I say. "Why didn't we drown?"

"You gave it your best shot, but I wasn't about to let that happen." She sits back on her heels and brushes the dust from her fingers. "I pulled you out, and, believe me, it was no easy task. You were already really invested in your nap."

"It wasn't a nap. It was a tranquilizer."

She shrugs. "Same result."

"Was I still . . . you know . . . when you pulled me out?"

"Don't worry. I was careful not to touch your claws." She glances at the drag marks that I can see leading the few feet up from the water. "It would've been a *lot* easier if I hadn't had to worry about that." She looks back at me and blows out what sounds like a sigh of relief. "It's a good thing you didn't drown. I have no idea how I would've performed CPR on you."

I slowly get to my feet. My body sways. I'm still woozy. There's a monster headache threatening at the base of my skull.

Just as long as it doesn't turn me back into a monster.

My skin responds to the cold air blowing in across the lake, and I look down at my arm. There's no hair to rise with the goosebumps, but I feel my skin prickle in protest anyway. Brushing the fingers of my other hand over my arm, I watch the dust float to the sand. Then I sit down and pull off the boots.

"Sam? What are you doing?"

Standing, I unbutton the jeans and pull them down to my ankles. More gritty dust spills away from my skin. I yank my feet from the jeans and rush for the water. It's so cold it nearly takes my breath away. I yelp—a wonderfully human sound—and swear in delight as I plunge in up to my waist. I duck down, holding my breath, and pop back up like a cork, spraying water from my lips.

As I rub the last of the curse from my body, shivering so violently I can barely see straight, I feel my lips peel back in a smile. A real smile. I splash water on my face, running my fingers over the novelty of nose, ears, lips, and chin. My scalp is bare. There's not a hair anywhere on my body, actually. No eyebrows. No eyelashes. No pubes. And I don't care. I *don't care*. This, I can handle.

I sink down to my shoulders in the frigid water, where I don't seem to shiver so much in the cold air. Tegan watches from the shore, her arms wrapped around her middle. She must be freezing. She was in the lake, too. And it's November now. November first.

It's over.

With a giant whoop of laughter, I rise up and sprint out of the lake, dripping water everywhere, and grab Tegan up into my arms. She holds me just as tightly, pressing her lips into the space between my shoulder and neck.

"You did it," I say.

"What did I do?"

"Everything." I breathe in the scent of her damp hair and feel tears spring to my eyes again. Great. I'm not going to be one of those guys who cries all the time, am I?

"Okay." She pulls back and plants her hands on my chest. "But put your pants on, will you?"

I laugh and reach for my damp jeans, shaking the last of the dust from them. When I get them on and buttoned up, I turn to Tegan. Her expression makes my blood run cold. I whirl around just in time to see Dr. Grant run down a short flight of wooden steps and onto the beach.

When he sees me standing there with Tegan, he stops short and just stares. His gaze jumps between us, so fast it's almost comical. I take a step back, my bare feet sinking into the charcoal-dusted sand. Tegan slips her hand into mine, lacing our fingers together. For a split second, I panic . . . and then I remember that the claws are gone. I squeeze her hand, feeling the warmth spread between us.

"Where is he?" Dr. Grant asks. His voice is slow and deliberate, but hesitant, like he's not quite sure of what's going on, and he doesn't want to give anything away if he doesn't have to.

"Who?" Tegan's voice is so falsely innocent that I know Dr. Grant will never buy it.

"You know who I'm talking about. Sam. Where is he?"

"Where do you think he is?" she retorts. But I barely hear her. My attention focuses to a laser-like point on the second figure coming down the stairs. His gait is familiar. His hair is a little shorter, the hairline receded a bit. He wears glasses now, but . . .

He stops when he sees me, then suddenly turns away, pulling off his glasses and pressing his thumb and forefinger to his eyes as if to stanch the flow of tears. Dr. Grant turns, and the expression on his face changes from one of angry confusion to one of bewildered understanding.

"Who is that?" Tegan whispers. I can't answer. All I can do is watch as the man replaces the glasses on his face and walks toward me, carefully composing himself.

"Sam." The man's voice is strangled. His gaze sweeps over my face, coming to rest on my eyes. "You . . ."

"I what?"

"You have your mother's eyes." His chin, a mirror image of my own, wobbles with suppressed tears. He shakes his head. "I'm sorry, Sam. I'm so sorry. I know you can't forgive me. I just didn't know what to do."

"Forgive him for what?" Tegan whispers. "Sam, who is this?"

"My father." My voice is flat. My speech impediment makes me sound like a toddler, and suddenly all I want to do is act like one. Shout at this man. Scream at him. Throw sand. Kick his shins. Would it help? Maybe. But it would probably also get me thrown into the psych ward, and Dr. Grant would make sure they threw away the key.

I shake my head. Who's the real enemy here? Who kept me locked up for eleven years, unable to see the sky? Who cut off my wings and tail under the guise of being helpful?

Who fed me live rodents just to see if I would eat them? Who stripped me of my autonomy and held me captive and wouldn't let me leave?

As if he knows I'm thinking about him, Dr. Grant steps forward. "You're going to get hypothermia out here. Both of you. Sam, we need to get you back to the hospital so I can run some tests for—"

"No!" I shout. "No more tests. I'm not your guinea pig anymore. There's nothing wrong with me. And your tests would never find anything, anyway. They never did."

"Sam," he says, talking slowly as if I'm a moron, "you are still my patient."

"I'm not sick."

"We don't know if you are. This is . . . This is unprecedented."

"That doesn't give you the right to experiment on me."

"Sam!" He looks like I just slapped him. I can't tell if he's genuinely shocked, or if this is more for my father's benefit.

I turn to my father, who's been staring at me in silence. He unzips his jacket and pulls it off.

"Come here, Sam." When I don't move, he walks forward and holds the jacket out to help me into it. Tegan lets go of my hand. I miss her warmth instantly, but the fleecy lining of the jacket starts to compensate a little. Dad zips it up and places his hand on my shoulder as he looks into my eyes. "I *am* sorry. More sorry than you'll ever know. I could have protected you. I could have stopped all of this before it ever started. But I didn't, and I will regret it for the rest of my life."

"Mom—" I begin, but he cuts me off with a shake of his head.

"I don't blame you for that. It was an accident. Like I said, I was the one who could have prevented all of this." He squeezes my shoulder. "I don't blame you, all right, Sam?"

I nod slowly, and Dad gives me a sad smile.

"Come on. Let's get you someplace warm."

"No." Dr. Grant shakes his head. "I'm afraid I can't allow that. He's under my care, and he might be a danger to—"

"Sam's a danger to no one, and you know it." Dad's voice is weary but defiant. "You've always known it. I stayed away because you told me there was no way of knowing what would happen, no way of knowing if what he had was contagious. You knew it wasn't. I knew it wasn't. But I listened to you. And that is something else I will regret for the rest of my life." He puts an arm around my shoulders. "You're not going to take any more of his life away from him, Dr. Grant."

"Do I need to call the police?"

"Go ahead," Tegan says. "Call them. And I'll tell them how you shot Sam with a tranquilizer dart. Do you know when it kicked in? Guess." She doesn't give him time to. "It was when we were over the middle of the lake. We could've drowned. Sam almost did."

Dr. Grant's face is nearly white with fury. "That was a necessary measure. I was trying to protect *you*, young lady."

"I didn't need protecting. Not from Sam." She reaches for my hand again and gives it a fierce squeeze. "If there's one person on this beach that I need protecting from—that we all need protecting from—it's probably you." She gives a violent shudder and clings to my arm. Her lips have taken on a bluish tinge.

"Can we go home now?" I ask my father as I pull Tegan against my side.

Dad nods. "Yes. Yes, Sam, we can go home now." He reaches into the front pocket of his jacket and pulls out a cell phone. "I'll have to call us a ride, though, because I'm not going anywhere with him." He can't even look at Dr. Grant as he says this.

The three of us walk up the steps, two with half-frozen legs and shivering limbs, one only slightly chilly in his thin plaid shirt. We don't look back at the man on the beach. We pay him no attention as he storms up the steps in a fury, gets into his fancy car, and drives away. I watch him disappear from my life, taillights fading into the mist, and I start to cry again. This time, there are two people to hold me, to warm me as we stand on an unfamiliar street, waiting for a car that will bring me, finally, into an unfamiliar but wonderfully normal life.

I'm so excited I could chirp.

About the Author

Nissa Harlow wanted to be a writer from the time she was a small child, but it took a while before she finally did anything about it. In the meantime, she worked as a volunteer day-camp counsellor, a movie extra, and a digital-photo editor. She even once worked on a conveyor belt in a chocolate factory (which was as stressful—and delicious—as it sounds). These days, she lives in British Columbia, Canada and writes the types of stories she wants to read.

nissaharlow.com

Also by Nissa Harlow

www.ingramcontent.com/pod-product-compliance
Lightning Source LLC
Chambersburg PA
CBHW051146190726
48290CB00006B/2013